STERLING'S REASONS

Joey Light

KISMET is a trademark of Meteor Publishing Corporation

Copyright © 1991 Georgia Ann Damon

Cover Art Copyright © 1991 Tom Hallman

All rights reserved.

Neither this book nor any part may be reproduced or transmitted in any form or by any means, electronic or mechanical, including photocopying, recording, or by any information storage and retrieval system, without permission in writing from the Publisher. Meteor Publishing Corporation, 3369 Progress Drive, Bensalem, PA 19020.

First Edition

ISBN 1-878702-46-7

A KISMET™ Romance

METEOR PUBLISHING CORPORATION
Bensalem, Pennsylvania

JOEY LIGHT

Joey Light is married to her high school sweetheart, has four sons and lives in the foothills of Western Maryland on a small farm. Joey has a predilection for a magical 150-year-old log cabin, full moon nights, music from classical to Croce, and retrieving newborn foals from knee-deep muddy pastures.

ONE

"The cop who killed his partner?"

"That's the one. Name's Joe Timothy MacDaniels." He pushed the Washington *Post* across the desk to her. He watched her over his steepled fingers. "Don't give me that little-girl 'good grief' look of yours, Sterling. Think about it. The preliminary report states he has no family. Is he going to quit the force; start a new life? End the old one? Is he going to wind up in a nut house because he's alone? The newspaper doesn't give that kind of information."

Sterling picked up the paper and studied the picture of the man on the front page under the headline LT. ACCI-DENTALLY KILLS HIS PARTNER. The face was worldly, the eyes were clear and direct. A thick mustache hid his top lip. She wouldn't exactly call it a cold face, but she could call it aloof. Of course it was a file photo. She wondered what those eyes looked like now. And the hint of a smile would be gone. The handsomeness might be hidden beneath lines of pain. God, a thing like that,

7

Sterling couldn't imagine it. It was a mistake, a bad one, but definitely an accident. She had read about it. She had watched it on TV as she forced down a piece of cold pizza during the late news.

"He's been put on administrative leave," she read.

"Read on. He's pulled himself out of the picture for a while. Get out there. Find out what you can."

When Sterling hesitated a moment longer than Mr. Ramsburg thought she should, he added, "How many years have you been working for me now, Sterling?"

"Five, sir."

"How many times have we failed to be able to do something constructive? How many times has there been no reason to intervene?"

"Out of about thirty cases, none, sir." She smiled then, for she knew what he was getting at. "Sometimes I just wish I knew what drives you. What makes you do this? I think it's wonderful, you know that . . . Where would I be without you, but . . ."

"When I stop, you become unemployed, Sterling. So you better just sit back for the ride. I take good care of myself and the money . . ." He shrugged, gesturing it away, "I don't need it and others do. Certainly not that money-grubbing so-called family of mine." He grimaced, remembering. "Tossed me from one to the other when I became orphaned. Different darn story when I made something out of myself. I just make more money to aggravate them. I have more than one person should." The twinkle in his eye was hidden as he looked down to straighten the cuffs of his shirt.

"Don't worry about me, child. Just continue to do your job as well as you have been. You have a gift. You can see into people. You can pick up on feelings others can't. Like the family that was burned out. I would simply have built them a new house." He sipped from a full brandy snifter. "You got to know them and told me that they needed to be relocated back to where most of their family lived. So they miraculously found a job opening and a house in their hometown. It was so much more effective that way. Your job is to find out, and my job is to enable. Together we make a darn good team."

"You've given more people a second chance, a new perspective, a clean slate and a shot at a real life, and all this without anyone knowing where it came from or why. It just burns inside me to let them know."

"Well, it doesn't burn inside me, and since it's my money that does the job, you can't tell them." His entire face wrinkled into a smile. "Gets you, doesn't it, Ster?"

She had to shake her head and smile at the man. "Somewhere along the way, someone gave you a helping hand or a another chance. Will you ever tell me about it?"

He leaned over his desk a little. "No, you'll never learn my life story, young lady. Don't you know by now that I thrive on secrets?"

Sterling replaced the newspaper on the corner of the huge cherry desk and looked at Mr. Ramsburg. Fatigue creased his forehead and weakened his eyes. It was nearing four o'clock, and Sterling often wondered where he got the drive to continue with his work at seventy years of age. His hands remained steepled under his chin as he watched her. His suit was a fine gray pinstriped double-breasted wool. He dressed with immaculate care. His tie was dark gray with a hint of maroon running through it. His hair was white and thin. His eyes, though tired, remained direct and challenging.

Smiling indulgently, Sterling assured him. "I'll fine-tune my magic wand and make arrangements to get to D.C. right away." She stood up, moving her pad and pen to her right hand. Smoothing the skirt of her navy-blue suit, she moved toward the office door.

"Already been made. He's on a sabbatical of sorts in North Ocean City, so it will be a little farther to travel. Nancy has your tickets and the investigator's reports. You leave at five-thirty tomorrow," he paused for effect, "on a plane."

"I'm to fly?" She stopped with her hand on the brass knob.

Mr. Ramsburg smiled. "Yes. When are you going to conquer your fear of the big metal bird? No other way to travel, dear girl. Now shoo. Get your things in order. And stop sighing and get home and pack. It's beautiful in Ocean City. Take some time to enjoy yourself, but remember, this chap may need our help right this very minute. And, Sterling . . ."

She stopped with the door open to the outer office and looked back at him. "Wear your blue jeans. That suit makes you look too staid, and you're too young and beautiful to look so solemn." He took in her bright tawny-gold eyes and her light-brown hair. "And a bathing suit. Two-piece. You need some color." He winked, and she raised a brow then let herself out of his office.

By six-thirty that evening her bags were packed and set by the door. She would liked to have taken a train. Or a pack mule, she thought as she shoved the suitcase back against the wall. He knew she hated flying and that's exactly why he made her do it.

She gathered Edison, her gray long-haired cat, in one hand and picked up the bag with his food and favorite toys in it in the other one as she headed across the hall to Mrs. Murphy's apartment. She knocked on the door with the toe of her shoe.

Mrs. Murphy swung the door wide. "Come on in, my dear. Hello, Edison." She took the gray cat from Sterling and rubbed his whiskered face against hers. "How are you, Edison? You pretty boy," she crooned.

Sterling ambled past them to set the bag of food on the sink top. "I certainly appreciate your taking him again this time. I think he's more your cat than mine anyway. I shouldn't be longer than two or three weeks."

"Not to worry. He's company for an old lady like me. I still have the litter box here and a whole new bag of litter. The green kind. He likes that the best." She took the cat to her big raggedy overstuffed chair by the window and sat down, arranging him in her lap. Edison looked up at Sterling with an expression that told her he would never forgive her for this. Again.

"You're a godsend, Mrs. Murphy. I'll see you when I get back. And thank you."

She looked away from the cat just long enough to study Sterling. "That company you work for is too hard on you. Always sending you here and there. Don't they see how skinny you are? Last time you were away for two months and now they're sending you away again. Did you ever think of changing jobs? My niece, Lori, has a wonderful job waitressing down at Matt's. Makes good money, too, and doesn't have to leave her home for days and months at a time." She pointed a bony finger toward Sterling. "You consider it while you're on this trip. Promise me, girl."

Sterling merely smiled. Mrs. Murphy's stockings were rolled down to her ankles. The flowery dress was protected by an apron hooked around her neck and tied at her ample waist. "I promise." With a wave, Sterling pulled the door shut behind her, and then took a minute to rest her back on it. *I'm not skinny*, she thought, and looked down at herself. *Well*, she sighed inwardly, *not real skinny*.

Moments later, propped up on the couch against several pillows, the radio playing softly in the kitchen, Sterling broke the seal on the first of the four envelopes. She would use the contents to make herself familiar with this Joe MacDaniels.

As she read, she nibbled on pretzels and drank Diet Coke. He was forty-five; born in Indiana to Lee and Ann MacDaniels. He was raised on a farm, went to school when it pleased him. Enlisted and spent three years in the Army, one in Vietnam. Decorated twice; the Silver Star and the Bronze Star for Valor. His parents were killed in an accident while he was in-country. No brothers or sisters. No family was listed at all. Nothing out of the ordinary. His police record was clean, though he seemed to be a bit of a rule-stretcher. He got the job done and done well. He'd accomplished many arrests and convictions. Reading between the lines she got the idea that he was his own man. He seemed afraid of nothing. She had an image of an in-charge type of person who was highly respected. She idly wondered what made a man so devoted to something, so channeled.

The other envelopes contained his employment record, his service record, dozens of newspaper clippings, and a synopsis. No commendations. A few mild reprimands. One investigation. All cleared. There was a list of former addresses along with a list of references and a few pages of comments by the investigators. It seemed he had rented an old beach cottage in North Ocean City. It was all so routine, Sterling shrugged lazily and snuggled deeper into the pillows. She fell sound asleep. The pretzel slid from her hand to the rug. The radio continued to play.

She had forgotten to set the alarm clock and her mood reflected it. Clutching a suitcase, with an overnighter slung over her shoulder, she ran down to the cab that had just slid to a halt at the curb.

"The airport, and hurry." She tossed an absent smile at the driver. "There's an extra ten in it for you if I make the flight in one piece. We only have an hour and a half."

She knew it was a mistake as soon as he peeled away from the curb and butted into traffic with a hell-bent look on his face. Sterling let her head drop back as she reached up to massage her neck. The couch had cramped her muscles and all the hurrying and rushing hadn't helped. Nasty fingers of tension gripped her shoulders, sneaking higher to press on her temples.

At the airport, she spotted a snack bar and bought a

Coke to wash down the Dramamine. Double checking to be sure she had packed her Hershey bar in her purse, she sprinted toward the gate. She was in time. Slowing down, she got in line to board, then drew a deep breath, pulled her tickets from her briefcase, and handed them to the attendant. Suppressing the familiar flutter of panic, she followed the other passengers down the jetway.

Her ticket placed her in the window seat with a fat man and a little girl as her companions. She watched the activity around the plane and tried to even her breathing. She had flown many places for Mr. Ramsburg, but it never got any easier. Once she was up, the tension eased a little until they hit an air pocket or turbulence, then she was all tight again. She guessed it had something to do with the fact that she was totally out of control, at someone's mercy from the time she passed through the plane door till the time she got off . . . and she liked having the control herself.

The taxi to takeoff was uneventful. She unwrapped her chocolate bar. The build up of speed was almost fascinating. She broke off a square. The roar of the engines increased, and she felt the indescribable lurch in her stomach as the wheels left the ground. When the plane dragged and then finally lifted she popped the candy in her mouth and chewed. Breathing wasn't a priority when one was chewing. The fat man leaned over her and watched the dropping landscape. Sterling kept her eyes on the book she brought along to make her look nonchalant. She saw no words, only a blur. Another bite on the candy bar and they were leveling off. The attendants began to stir. Good, she thought. A drink would be coming soon and she needed it to take more air-sickness medicine.

Sterling took this chance to force herself to relax. Her thoughts wandered back to the beginning of this job. Mr. Ramsburg had repeatedly sent her first class. She finally convinced him that she didn't like the fact that the attendent watched her and waited on her hand and foot. It only served to make her more nervous. Against his better judgment, he let her take business class so she could be less conspicuous if she threw up. He was as good to her as his nature allowed him to be. She recalled another time he had been patiently generous toward her. A vehicle had been part of the deal when he hired her. After he asked her which one she wanted, she had thought a minute and said that she would like to rent, by the month. That way she could drive everything there was to drive. She remembered how he had thrown his head back, laughed, and said, "You and I are going to get along just fine, young lady." And so they had. Sterling was glad when the stewardess stopped the beverage cart beside their row.

An hour and a half later the wheels touched the ground and Sterling sighed in relief. She shoved the last square of the Hershey bar into her mouth and let it melt.

She was driven from the airport to a small, dilapadated but nicely furnished cottage next to where MacDaniels was reported to be staying. The limo was obvious and she wanted to be alone as soon as possible so she helped unload her bags and sent the smiling driver on his way.

The cottage was one thing, but the ocean was another. She ran to the deck and let the wind rip through her hair. The tide was up and the water was rolling furiously. She loved it. She had forgotten how much she adored the sea. This was going to be gravy after all. Then she thought about Joe. Was the atmosphere here helping what he must be feeling? What exactly was he feeling?

Looking to her left, she studied the cottage next to hers. It was old and weatherbeaten, too. Sand had blown up on the first two steps leading to the deck. As hers did, the cottage looked slightly off square and dangerously close to collapsing. Jammed into the sandy hillside, the houses reminded her of two giant spiders with their legs planted solidly in the sand, standing guard or waiting. Simply waiting, she decided.

So this was North Ocean City. Away from the mobs of tourists, away from the boardwalk with its openmouthed stores. A short distance off the tip of the steps, the water stretched for miles. She wondered idly exactly where she would land if she set sail from here and steered in a straight line. Always fascinated by answers, she made a mental note to check a map.

Walking around the deck, she inspected everything. It was quiet here except for the roar of the water and the hum of the breeze. No horns blaring, tires screeching, or people rushing here and there. She hoped they would have a hurricane or something wild during her stay. The more fury the water rolled with, the better. Smiling, she tried to take in everything at once. This was exciting and different. The gulls swooped overhead calling a welcome.

Anxious to unpack and take a long walk on the beach, Sterling moved toward her suitcases. Then stopped. The heck with unpacking, she told herself. She chucked her shoes where she stood and ran down the steps. The sand was warm and gave under her light weight. She wriggled her toes in it as she took long strides.

It was nearly ninety degrees. The vicious, glaring sun beat hard on the shore. It was almost one o'clock. Her stomach rumbled. She looked up toward Joe's cottage as she passed but saw no movement. Maybe he was taking a nap. She couldn't believe anyone would be inside for any other reason when there was so much to see and experience. And her naps would be taken on the deck.

She walked for a mile. The beach became even more isolated and weeds jutted here and there giving it a primitive feel. Many times she had to detour around old, rotting boards, the remains of walkways or gazebos long lost to the ravages of time and never rebuilt. Maybe the owners had moved on to another beach or simply gone back to the city.

The tang of salt was everywhere. She could almost taste the air. She found seashells along the way and filled the

pockets of her blue sundress. Stepping back to catch one
that was rolling to shore, she caught the heel of her foot
on a rock and scraped it. "Ouch," she exclaimed.

Plunking herself down, she examined the wound.
Blood. Phooey. She headed back to her cottage, carefully,
on the tiptoes of that foot. Now it was time to find out how
thorough Mr. Ramsburg's people had been in stocking her
cupboard.

Sterling walked a long way and was tired when she
finally hobbled home. She was almost past Joe's place
when she looked up and saw him leaning on the railing.

"Hello there, neighbor," she called up to him, shading
her eyes with her hand.

He stared at her a moment before pushing away from
the railing. Well, so much for friendliness, she thought to
herself as she limped on over to her stairs.

No peroxide. No iodine. Not even a small tube of first-
aid cream. But there *was* tea. She ran water in the kettle
and put it on the stove.

In the bathroom, she held her foot under the shower
water. Closer examination showed her it was a pretty deep
gash and required some attention. An idea struck her.
What better way to meet the surly man next door? Sometimes on these cases she would map a plan. Other times
she would wing it. She figured it would be the latter for
this one. Sterling brewed her tea and took time to enjoy
it before crossing the sand.

She wondered briefly if she should climb the sand dune
and knock on what served as a front door or simply climb
the stairs to the deck. The deck was closest.

Reaching the top, she stopped. He was there, just inside
the open glass door, stretched out on a bright, flowered
couch. A bottle of vodka tipped precariously against a
stack of paperback books. His arm was flung over his
eyes. She assumed he was asleep. Before she could decide
whether to call out to him or come back later, he moved.

He didn't sit up, he merely removed the arm from over his eyes. "What do you want?"

His voice was low and smooth, and a little thick with sleep. She hesitated again. He sat up on the couch. Because he was stripped to the waist she saw that his chest was solid and his shoulders were broad. A thick mat of dark hair dipped to a V where his belted Levi's began. But it was his eyes that struck her. Winded her. It wasn't just the unique honey-brown color. There were strong emotions lurking beneath, darkening like shadows on silk. His voice, like his heavy lids, made her wonder if he had had way too much to drink or if he really had been sleeping. Either way, he was striking. She was reminded of steel. Of sparks when two rocks were struck together. Of a grizzly bear being disturbed in his den.

Interested and amused, she had to smile. His hair had grown too long to be stylish and his mustache needed trimming. He looked disheveled and disturbed. And ticked off.

She found her voice. "Peroxide," and almost lost it again when he stood up. Even with his shoes off, he was tall. Over six feet. She had to look up to meet his eyes. His mouth was full and sensuous even though at the moment it was pressed in a tight, annoyed line. Her gaze dropped to his tight-fitting jeans and took in the muscled thighs and the wear to the right knee section.

"What for?" He glared at her, sweeping a hand through his hair.

"Cut my foot. Anything antiseptic will do. I hated to bother you, but we seem to be the only ones down this end and . . ."

He took her none too gently by the wrist, plunking her down on the couch. The shells in her pockets scraped together. Taking her foot in his hand he turned her heel toward him slightly so he could have a look. Without a word, he reached for the vodka bottle and tipped it end up. The few drops that were left in it rolled over the open skin and burned like lightning.

On a yelp, she jumped up. She tried to stand but lost her balance and fell back on the couch again. "That burns."

He glowered at her impatiently. "You said anything antiseptic would do, and it did. Now, is that all?"

She got up this time, and he took her place. He picked up a book as he did, but she noticed it was upside down. He was dismissing her. But she wasn't ready to leave yet. While she looked around, the burning subsided a little. The place was a mess. Clothes everywhere, piles of dirty and stacks of clean. Empty cardboard cartons and boxes proved he frequented the fast-food joints. The furniture was sparse and only what was necessary. Old raggedy curtains hung this way and that, one rod completely off the hook. There wasn't a TV set or a stereo in the room. Books and magazines littered a coffee table and the floor. Overflowing ashtrays, many of them, sat here and there.

Remembering her manners, Sterling offered, "Except to say thank you."

"Don't." He pretended to read the book.

"Mr. McDaniels, I . . ."

The book hit the floor and he shot up to stare at her. "The minute I saw that fine, fancy car this morning, I had you made. You're a plant from IAD. Damn them." Disgusted, he stormed to the door and braced his hand against it.

"IAD? What's that?"

"Don't play games with me. They figured they'd send some sweet-looking piece down here to keep an eye on me. To find out what they could." He swung around to face her, his anger darkening his eyes. "Well, it won't work. I've already told them everything. Now get on out of here."

She pulled herself up to her full five feet five inches. "I'm not with IAD, whatever that is."

"Then how'd you know my name?" He came close, and she could feel the power that moved in him.

"It's been in every newspaper . . . with pictures. Though I must say your appearance has changed somewhat, your hair has grown and your . . ."

"Bull." He steamed toward the kitchen area and swung back to accuse her again. "Then you're a reporter here to get a scoop. Probably from one of those raggy gossip magazines."

Slumping back on the couch, he let his head rest on his hands.

Her heart went out to the man. He might bellow and stomp and speak roughly, but she saw passed that. She sat down beside him. When she did, he looked up at her as if unable to believe she hadn't run to the deck and down the stairs.

"I assure you I'm not any of those things." She faced his gruff expression. "I'm here on sort of a rest. I need one. Yes, rest and relaxation." She nodded to herself as much as to him. She was pleased with her impromptu excuse. "I work in New York and the boss sent me here because I was becoming stagnant. We're neighbors, that's all." She shrugged, hoping a simple explanation would be enough. "And I recognized you the minute you scowled at me. Want to go out to dinner tonight?"

He sat back on the couch and studied her with steady, unamused eyes. She could tell that getting this man to trust her was going to be the first big hurdle to clear.

He began talking very slowly as if to be sure she understood every word. "I came here to be alone. I don't want any neighbors. I don't want to have dinner with a stranger, or with anyone I know for that matter. If you know who I am, then you know what I did."

"Yes." She sat back next to him and noticed a strange low charge of electricity start in her arm and travel to the pit of her stomach. "I know. And I'm very sorry it happened. It must be terrible for you, but dinner won't alter any of the facts, and I'm starved. From the looks of things," she waved her arm in the direction of the trash, "you haven't been eating well yourself. I don't like to dine alone. Come on, no place fancy, and I'll treat." After a moment, she flashed a smile at him.

He seemed to have come to a conclusion. Sterling could see the muscles working in his jaw.

Abruptly, he stood up. Grabbing the empty vodka bottle, he pitched it against the wall viciously. Glass shattered, sending shards of it skittering across the floor to mix with the sand near the sliding door.

Sterling jolted, startled.

Raking his hand through his hair, he wheeled around to face her. "You're not a reporter and you claim you're not with Internal Affairs. Then who the hell are you?"

She looked from the mess on the floor to the man towering in front of her. Cautious yet resolved, she stood, losing some of the patience she had been testing. "Sterling Powell. I'm thirty years old, I work in New York. I'm not married. I'm here on a vacation that started out badly, but I'm determined to straighten that out. I want dinner, Mr. McDaniels, and I want you to go with me."

"Sterling . . ." He tested her name. "Why do you want to have dinner with me?" His eyes traveled the length of her and back up.

She headed for the door, carefully avoiding the broken glass. "It's almost three now. How about six-thirty? That'll give me time to unpack and take a bath. I had a rotten start this morning, a worse flight, and now I find I have a troll for a neighbor. So, think of it as an act of mercy. You're a policeman. Look at it as your duty, if you must." She flashed another smile at him and was gone.

He stood there a full five seconds. "What the hell was that?" he questioned the thin air. Whirling, he flung himself back on the couch and muttered, "An act of mercy . . . look at it as your duty? A cold day in hell!"

TWO

He was bored enough to waste one evening on the broad. After all, his social calendar wasn't *that* full. Wiping the steam from the shower off his mirror, he sneered at himself. Leaning his hands on the sink, he examined what he saw. His eyes were darkened by shadows underneath. His face was almost gaunt. He looked like hell. He sure felt like hell. He ran a hand down his rib cage and his flat stomach. Besides, he hadn't had a decent meal since he'd arrived. Hadn't wanted one. Still didn't. Joe slapped aftershave on his face from a nearly empty plastic bottle. He ignored it when he bumped it and it fell on the floor to twirl into a corner.

Naked, he stalked from the bathroom to his room and rummaged through the clothes he'd thrown in a suitcase before he left. He grabbed black jeans from the pile and pulled them on. He could play along with her until he found out what she was up to. He peeled a shirt from a hanger and shrugged it on. He was good at pretending to do one thing while actually doing another. Yanking a sport coat from the post of his bed, he flung it on.

In the living room, he searched for his keys, growing frustrated with the clutter. One swipe of his hand cleared the end table of several magazines, an ashtray, and his keys. He grabbed them and stuck them in his pocket. After checking his wallet and assuring himself he had cash, he steamed to the door and jerked it open. He wasn't a man to be tricked or manipulated. And she'd know that before this evening was over.

She heard him start his Jeep and drive it to the front of her cottage. She glanced in the mirror one more time and then pushed through the front door. It was precisely six-thirty.

"Hi," she said brightly, and slid onto the seat. So, he had showered and shaved. She could smell the soap and the spicy aftershave. He had put on a light gray corduroy sport jacket over a black shirt and black jeans. In short, he looked wonderful.

"Where do you want to go?" He slammed the Jeep in first and spun out in the sand onto the asphalt road without waiting for her answer.

"Anywhere they serve big burgers and greasy french fries. I love junk food, you might as well know that now." She sized him up. "I figure you for a steak and potatoes man. Gravy all over, right?"

He looked straight ahead and drove. Idle chatter wasn't his way. Not before and certainly not now. He turned west and headed toward the highway. He'd find someplace decent and get this over with.

She cast a quick glance at him. He hadn't even said she looked pretty and she had deliberately put on her black silk slacks with the white blouse and black lace around the cuffs.

He remained silent as she made comments on the passing landscape or the shops and restaurants. He turned right over a wooden bridge and then into a parking lot half full of cars. The gravel grated beneath the tires as he came to an abrupt halt.

She opened her own door thinking he wouldn't do it, only to almost collide with him when he came around to do just that. She let him take the door and hold it for her. Sterling saw that his eyes checked out her legs as she got out. She ignored what was a natural, manly thing to do. Tucking her arm through his, she walked up the wooden ramp with him. It was there again. That charge of electricity, like rubbing a balloon against her hair. So, he was a good-looking man and it was only natural for her to respond to him. He had a good build and, despite his surliness, she had already honed in on a gentleness that lurked just beneath the surface. He was going through a bad time and she had to be patient with him.

The restaurant was wonderful. It was as if she had been propelled back in time to the old, serious fishing days. Nets hung from the ceiling full of all kinds of shells. Fish were mounted on the walls. The lights were low; the music slow. An apple-cheeked man led them to a table next to the window. It was covered with a blue linen cloth and set with gleaming silverware. The candle that glowed in the middle was a miniature ship's lantern.

Idly running her finger around the rim of the waiting coffee cup, Sterling commented cheerfully, "This is wonderful. Have you been here before? Look at the ropes and the shells. Aren't they the strangest wall hangings? Sort of a collage of pieces of wood painted different colors."

He sat back and ignored the menus being placed in front of them.

"Would the Mr. and Mrs. like a drink before dinner?" the waiter asked.

She didn't miss the narrowing of Joe's eyes before he ordered a vodka martini for himself and a Salty Dog for the lady.

As the waiter walked away she leaned forward and whispered, "I would have prefered a Coke, but that's okay. What is a Salty Dog?"

He lipped a cigarette out of the pack and lit it with an expensive gold lighter. "Smoke?"

"I don't mind."

"No, do you?"

"Oh, no. Did once, with my brother. Got sicker than a dog. I like this place, Mr. MacDaniels." Happily, she scanned the menu. "I'm going to have the Gangplank Burger. What are you ordering?"

"Some answers. What's your game, lady?"

Okay, she could be tough, too. "Look, MacDaniels." She lowered the menu and glared at him over the top of it. "If all you want is to play twenty questions with me, do it later. All I want is a nice restful dinner, with a relaxed companion."

This broad has left the realm of reality, he thought. He shook his head, slightly and wondered again at his decision to come here with her. He could be home now, stretched out on that couch . . . doing what? Anything he wanted to. But none of that was what he wanted to be doing. Everything was wrong. Everything was destroyed. By his own hand.

He drew a long breath and forced a smile. He planned on getting some information. He'd try the easy way first.

She wasn't prepared for the transformation a mere curling of his lips did to his face. He went from being handsome to being gorgeous. From foreboding to dangerous. From interesting to intriguing. She let her eyes linger on his smirk.

"For now, no more questions. But later I want answers." His eyes burned directly on hers over the smile and Sterling felt waves of anticipation roll through her. Anticipation of what she didn't know, but it was definitely there.

By the time the waiter took their orders, Sterling was glad to see that MacDaniels had forced himself to relax. He was actually trying to appear to be enjoying himself. When Sterling looked out the window all she could see was their reflections. They looked wonderful together. His dark, powerful look and her gentle, sunny one. Her eyes caught his in the glass and held. There was no smile now. He was back to that thoughtful look. It had a power to it all its own. She felt it clear down to her toes. She was saved by the approach of the waiter bringing their plates.

As she had predicted, he had steak, potatoes, and gravy. To her delight, her burger had to be cut in half and pressed down to be bite-size. The fries smelled delicious, and she dipped one of them in the side order of hot cheddar cheese she had asked for.

Oh, she had enjoyed the Salty Dog but she loved this. She groaned in delight as she put a cheese-laden fry in her mouth. "Oh, this is so good. Want a taste?"

He simply looked at her over his steak so she peeled the burger apart and shook some salt and pepper on it. "I guess not. Some other time, though. You don't know what you're missing." She threw him a smile as she steered the food toward her mouth.

"How can anyone who enjoys eating so much stay so skinny?"

It was the first civilized statement he had made since she met him, so she ignored his reference to her body and said, "I walk a lot. Besides, I just refuse to put on weight. Metabolism or something. And I work hard. I don't get to eat like this as often as I would like. How's your steak?"

"It'll sustain life."

"A man ought to enjoy food more than that. Just what do you do for entertainment, Mr. MacDaniels? I didn't even see a TV in your cottage."

"Read. Walk. Swim. I don't need to be entertained."

"Wonderful. Then tomorrow we can swim after breakfast and walk before lunch."

He leaned forward over the table toward her. "What's this *we* stuff? I suppose *we* could read before going to bed, too."

She let that hang in the air. He was baiting her and she was not going to take it. He was using all his policeman brain cells on her. "If it suits you. But I'll have to take one of your books to my cottage. I didn't bring any."

He sipped his martini and watched her. She ignored him and ate her dinner, looking around and enjoying the atmosphere.

When she climbed in his Jeep she felt like a cat. She wanted to find a shadowy spot and go to sleep. He headed back toward the cottages.

"Oh, wait! Look, there's a doughnut shop. Stop a minute, will you, I want to get a box for the morning. What kind do you like?"

He wheeled the Jeep in the lot and braked to a sudden halt. He had managed to accomplish absolutely nothing tonight and he wanted his solitude back again. Anything to get her to shut up and go home. "Cinnamon twistees."

"Okay. I like the ones with the cream in the middle. Pure sugar. And the chocolate ones. Umm."

He put his hand on her shoulder and leaned his face close. "Just get the damn things."

She was putting a strain on him, and by now she figured that was what she needed to do so that he would put up with her. If she made it too easy, he would simply dismiss her. He didn't know it yet, but she could get a lot worse.

Back in the Jeep and heading home, she breathed deeply. "I thought I was full, but after smelling these, I don't know."

The fact that he laughed out loud surprised her; that he shook his head and did it again pleased her. Sterling tilted her head and looked at him. Satisfied, she relaxed in the seat. She could see her plan was working.

He let her out at her door. "Aren't we going to walk some of this off?" she challenged.

He looked at her and seemed to be making some sort of judgment. "Half an hour, in front of your steps. And, Powell, wear shoes."

She wore shoes. Bright yellow hightops. Her skimpy matching green shorts and top let the slightly cooling evening breeze caress her midsection. He was waiting for her when she jogged down the steps.

"I thought you said walk," he said irritably as he jogged to catch up and then fell in step beside her.

"Jog and then walk. So, Mr. MacDaniels, when are you going back?"

He was silent for a moment and then, without looking at her, he simply answered with another question. "Back to where?"

"The department. How long did you take off?" It felt good to run, and she turned her face toward the setting sun to feel the last strong rays subside.

"I'll answer one question when you answer one."

She heard his breathing become slightly labored. "Out of shape for a cop. Been laying around too long already. Okay, what's your question?"

"Who are you?"

"Lord, MacDaniels, we've already been through this. How about this. I'm a psycopath or an axe murderer. Like that better?"

They jumped over some driftwood. "Right. And I'm Magnum and this is Hawaii. Yeah, I could learn to live with fairy tales. That all you know about?"

"You skipped your answer. One question for one answer, not question for question. You set the rules. Now play by them."

He sent her a dissolving look, but she just smiled at him.

"I'm not going back." He looked out to sea as they ran.

This took her by surprise. Granted, she didn't know much about him yet, but she didn't figure him for a quitter. "I don't like that answer."

"Why, because it puts a short end to your story?"

She was slowing down because she realized he was tiring. "No, I just didn't figure you for it."

He stopped and jerked her around by the arm. "Just

what did you figure me for? Why do you act like you know everything there is to know about me? Talk, or we go back and you stay away from me altogether.''

She bent over and took a few long breaths. ''Not supposed to stop dead. Slow down first and then walk until your pulse and breathing are normal.''

He put his hands on her shoulders and straightened her up. ''You're making me mad. You don't want to do that.''

The feel of his hands biting into her flesh was not all unpleasant. His eyes were cold and barely controlled as he looked deep into hers.

''I'm no threat to you, Joe MacDaniels. So stop acting like I am. Are you going to be suspicious of everyone you come in contact with, or just me?''

He continued staring as his breathing became normal. He searched her face for an answer. Found none. ''I don't believe you. You were sent here by somebody to do a story or to dig for more information . . . or simply to keep an eye on me.''

She shook her head. ''Consider yourself that important, do you? Look, I recognized you the minute I saw you. That's all. I'm tired of defending my being here. I'm here and I'm staying. Get used to it.''

He released her then, slowly. ''I'll find out what your game is, lady. I was a cop, a good cop, for a long time.''

She turned and headed back toward the cottages. ''And you're going to let it all go for nothing? Oh, look, this shell is perfect.''

She bent to pick it up and examine it in the failing light.

His voice softened involuntarily. She took such great pleasure from such small things. ''It's from my personal collection,'' he teased automatically. ''I keep them scattered out here so everyone can enjoy them.'' His dark, troubled eyes found hers as she smiled easily up at him.

''Can I have this one, Mr. MacDaniels?'' She held it toward him for his approval and played out the game.

He looked down at her hand and then back to her eyes.

He merely folded her fingers over the shell with his own and let their hands stay linked for a moment. "You can have it." If he'd been burned he could have stood the touch much easier. He shoved his hand in his pocket and turned away.

As they began the walk back she couldn't help but think about the sensation that traveled from their joined hands in her heart. She knew this man needed a friend, and she was going to be that friend, no matter what he wanted.

Hands linked behind her, Sterling ventured, "I love old movies, you know, Bogart and Becall, Tracy and Hepburn. I brought along *Casablanca* and *Key Largo*. My cottage is equipped with a TV and a VCR. Feel like watching them with me?"

"I don't watch television."

"This isn't television. This is art."

"It's that stupid romantic stuff." They were nearing the cottages now and they could see the lights they left burning. He looked up at his and then over toward hers.

"You think romance is stupid?" she questioned incredibly. "Oh, well, maybe it is," she shrugged, "but there's a lot of adventure in the films, too."

"Don't need adventure. I need sleep and vodka. And quiet."

"All right. Maybe tomorrow night. We could go to that place for dinner again. I really loved it, Mr. MacDaniels. Thank you."

He was standing close. She could feel the very maleness of him. Sterling wanted to reach out and stroke his hair and promise him everything would be okay, but she knew he would shake off her touch and she wasn't at all sure it would be.

"The name's Joe." Sometimes it took less energy to give up or in or whatever. Anything to stop this senseless chatter. "I suppose it's going to be a lot easier on me if I just say, Fine, dinner tomorrow night . . . but I pay, we make it only long enough to fill our stomachs and be done with it.''

She clapped her hands together happily. ''Okay, we can switch off nights. But I can cook when I want to. One night I'll fix something for us here. We can sit on the deck and watch the sea gulls fly and the sun go down. I like to play poker. Surely you do that.''

He still had that maddening, sulky look on his face. She wanted to see the smile again. ''You really think you can come in here and alter my life? You're trying to tell me my solitude has just been sabotaged. I don't think so.''

''Oh, no. I like my alone times, too. I just hope they coincide with yours. For lunch tomorrow I could fix a tuna casserole and we could go swimming afterward.''

''Why do I feel like a kid at camp being given directions by the counselor? I still don't buy your flimsy story. But it's enough for tonight.'' When she turned to go, he caught her hand. ''Don't trust me. Don't drop that innocent look on me and *don't* push me too far.''

She returned his direct stare. She pretended to think a minute and then touched her finger to his cheek for a quick second. ''Thanks for the warning.'' She ran toward her cabin and up the stairs.

He was plucking at her heartstrings and he wasn't even trying. Oh, she hoped she wasn't going to start liking this guy too much. Sometimes she got very attached to the people she worked with and it made it so hard to go back to New York.

Inside the cottage she changed to a nightgown and took one doughnut on a paper plate to the couch. A flip of the switch and she was into *Key Largo*. Glad for the diversion, she stretched out and got lost in the plot.

When she woke up, the picture on the TV was lines and fuzz. Glancing at the clock, she found that it was midnight. Groaning because she had missed the last part of the movie, Sterling tramped over and clicked off the

TV and VCR. Turning out the last of the lights, she went to the deck and leaned on the railing, breathing deeply of the sweet sea air. The breeze had picked up and it was cooler now, but it felt good. She stood and watched the moonbeams dance off the ocean crest.

Ten minutes later she saw movement on the beach. She heard the faint click of the lighter and saw the glow at the end of the cigarette. In the flash of light, she could make out his face. Lord, what was he doing walking around this late at night? He had been exhausted when she left him.

Fear struck her heart. Could he be thinking of doing something harmful to himself? She was sure a man in his position would think of it and in the short time she had spent with him she figured him to be the type of man who could follow through with anything he decided on. Without thinking about how she was dressed, she hailed him.

"Joe. Hey, Joe. A midnight stroll is just the thing. Wait."

She heard his groan but ran down the steps anyway. Mr. Ramsburg would throttle her if anything happened to this guy before she had time to help him.

"What the hell do you think you're doing? It's the middle of the night, you're not dressed, and you're with a stranger at the edge of nowhere."

"Oh, yes, well, it's dark. I get restless sometimes, too, you know. Besides, you might be a stranger, but I don't consider you dangerous."

In one quick movement he had her in his arms. "Consider me dangerous." Her breath was jerked from her. In the age-old movement, he lowered his mouth to hers in a crushing kiss. She didn't flinch. She didn't want to. His mouth was warm and demanding and taking without asking. She had never been kissed like that before. She could have struggled. She could have tried to stop him. She could have. But she didn't. She leaned into him and, pulling her trapped arms free, wrapped them around his neck.

It was all flash and color. The bones left her body and

she gave in to the dizzying effect his lips had on hers. There was no sound, no ocean, no breeze. Only him. She felt so fragile in his strong arms, then powerful and then weak. He tasted of salt and tobacco, and too much vodka. Only the touch of his lips did this to her? Only the play of his mouth on hers? The moan she heard was her own as he broke the kiss.

"Damn you." He didn't usually act like this. What was she doing to him? It was her fault, he decided. "It's only because I've wondered what it would be like to do that since you burst into my living room. I didn't ask you to come here. Now get back up those steps and go to bed before I take you to mine. And about tomorrow. Forget it." He pointed with the fingers that held the cigarette. "Stay away from me." He didn't need to know who she was or what she was up to. He didn't need her around to make him feel worse than he already did.

He disappeared into the night and she heard the soft creak of the wood as he jogged up the stairs.

A sudden wind came off the ocean and chilled her thoroughly. She shivered and wrapped her arms around herself and headed for the warmth of her cottage. Her mind was whirling and her heart felt strangely empty. She couldn't sort out her feelings. She wanted to follow him and tell him to do it again so she could analyze this. But she knew he wasn't to be played with so lightly. He was alone. He was a virile man. She was a woman, and he had needs. This wasn't exactly the type of thing she had envisioned happening, but now she had to admit, she, too, had wondered what it would be like to be in his arms. Now that she knew, she wasn't at all sure she should have found out.

Maybe she was going about this all wrong. She shouldn't let her emotions wander. Of course that was easier said than done when it had been a habit all her life to go with what pleased her the most. She had figured it would get her into trouble now and again. She looked out to sea, brushing the long hair up off her neck to let the breeze play on her skin. She was cold but had no desire to go indoors. Sometimes she thought best on her feet, and it was so quiet here and yet so loud. The noise of the ocean was in stark contrast to the silence on the beach. It played around her ears.

She had to get him to relax, to trust her. He had to open up with his feelings and his desires for her to inform Mr. Ramsburg what would be the best thing for him. She let her hair float down around her shoulders. It would be morning soon, and she wanted to watch the sunrise. She had to get some sleep. Turning to go back up the stairs to her deck, she thought she saw the faintest glow of a cigarette from his deck. She looked again but saw nothing.

In the short time she knew Joe McDaniels, she didn't figure him for the type that would stand in the darkness and watch a woman who thought she was alone. Why not? she thought. Bogart would have. Tracy would have. She took the steps two at a time and ran into the house. She was suddenly cold.

Joe hunkered against the chill night air. He watched her sprint into the house and then turned his gaze to the dark abyss of the sea. There was nothing out there . . . it was lifeless, it was empty, it was endless.

He pitched the cigarette over the deck and into the darkness. Casting one more look toward her cottage, he whirled on his heel and walked back into his house. It was just as lonely, just as bleak in there. Joe walked to the refrigerator, through the darkness from memory, and took the bottle of Tanqueray Sterling from the freezer. He poured a shot, watched the frost form on the glass, knocked it back, and tossed the empty glass on the counter. It rolled, balanced, and then fell on the floor.

THREE

It was the middle of September and the war of hot and cold air produced some hellish thunderstorms. When Sterling woke to thunder and lightning, she dressed quickly and ran to the deck. The water was rolling and pitching and smashing on the beach, very close to her steps. She loved it.

The heck with the sunrise. This was better. Much better. Feeling the chill in the air, Sterling turned back into the cottage to pull on a flannel shirt and jeans. Barefoot, she raced down the steps to stand dangerously close to the foaming sea. It was barely light, the time of day when morning and night battled for release. The icy spray of the water showered her. Lightning streaked across the sky, low and bright. A few seconds later the thunder rolled and cracked. The wind was fierce. Smiling, she stretched her arms up, turning her face to the oncoming storm.

"That's right. Stand out there like some damn lightning rod. Hope for a direct hit." Joe shook his head and ran a hand through his hair.

Though his voice was buffeted around by the wind, she heard him and laughed. Turning to look at him, she shouted back, wondering why he would care, "Isn't this wonderful?"

She watched him stomp down the steps, a frown drawing his brows together. The instant he reached her, he jerked her by the arm and dragged her back up the stairs into his cottage. This woman was not only infuriating, she was addlepated.

"That's really stupid. Only a fool would stand on the beach during a thunderstorm. You need someone to protect you from yourself. Watch the damn storm from in here. At least that way I'll know you haven't decided to take a boogie board out and ride the waves." He flicked his cigarette hard enough to send it out the doors and over the deck.

"I've only seen this once before." She stood by the sliding-glass door and watched as she talked. "I was a child and I was with my parents. Farther south, though, I think. I'd forgotten how beautiful it could be. And frightening."

"If it's frightening why were you standing out there, right on the edge of it?" He knew the answer.

She turned a smile on him. "It's scarier from that angle. You feel a part of it. There's the slightest chance of being carried away forever. Did you know that if you sailed a straight line from here you would land in Portugal? I looked it up."

He stirred something on the stove. "No, and I don't care."

Reluctantly, she moved away from the open door and into the kitchen area to see what he was doing. He was scrambling eggs, and badly. Peeking around from behind him, she asked, "What do you care about, Joe?"

"Nothing." *Not anymore*, he thought.

"You have to add a little more milk and you should've put a little butter in the frying pan first." She opened the refrigerator and, finding the milk, checked the date before gently nudging him aside and adding a little. Taking the fork from him she proceeded to fix the eggs. It was then that she heard the pitiful mewing sounds from the dark corner behind her.

Looking over her shoulder, she saw a box with three tiny kittens in it. She looked from the kittens to the back of the man braced against the doorjamb staring silently at the ocean. "Where in the world did the kittens come from?"

He didn't turn. "Your mother didn't tell you?"

She set the fork down and pulled the box out into the light. Two orange and one gray. They looked up toward her with unseeing, nearly newborn eyes. "Someone dropped them off?"

"I guess. Found them two days ago out front."

"And you're caring for them?" She was amazed . . . and touched.

"No, they're caring for me. You're burning the eggs," he added, provoked.

She returned to the skillet as he stalked back and shoved the box back in the corner.

"What do you feed them?"

"I was wondering the same thing myself. They licked a little milk off my fingers last night. Think they can handle the eggs?"

She laughed. "And I thought you were fixing breakfast for *us*. No, they most certainly cannot handle the eggs. Fix some toast, will you? I hate eggs by themselves. Then we'll have to go into town and find some doll bottles and baby formula." She took the skillet and flipped the eggs out onto two clean plates she'd found in the cupboard.

He burned the toast, then proceeded to scrape most of the black off over the sink. Joining him at the small dinette table, she noticed how haggard he looked. How long had it been since he had had a good night's sleep? "Are you all right?" she asked.

"Eat," he grunted.

"It's really a rotten breakfast. We could have gone to town. If you don't have much money, I have enough. What we ought to do is stock the fridge. We can do that while we shop for your babies."

He looked up at her then. There was a small crumb of toast in the corner of his mouth. His hair had fallen over his forehead. The night's growth of beard shadowed his chin and sculpted it to appear outlawish. His shirt was a mess. It was wrinkled and opened to his waist. She kept her eyes level with his so as not to look at where the dark hair traveled across his bare chest.

"They're not my babies," he objected bad-temperedly. "Just some stupid no-good strays that somebody dumped near my car. Probably hoped I would run over them. I should have. I thought I'd let them grow bigger and make rugs out of them."

She laughed then, good and hearty. "Oh, you don't fool me, Joe. You have a big heart beneath all that growling. It'll be fun to care for them."

"Good. Then take them to your place."

"No way. They're yours. But I'll help you now and then. It will give you something else to do besides brooding and drinking."

"I'll reserve the right to do whatever pleases me."

"To a point," she agreed and finished her charred toast.

"You mean last night?" He toyed with the food on his plate.

She set her fork down, contented. "No, I didn't mean last night, but now that you mention it, I guess it does include that. I was talking about the fact that it's time to get your life going again. You can't just live in limbo forever. It's been almost five weeks now. Why do you feel that punishing yourself will help anything?"

"Lord, a shrink." He bumped his elbow on the table. "I didn't think of that one." He rubbed the spot where a bruise was forming. "But who would send a shrink after me? There's nobody . . ."

"I look like a psychiatrist?" she chuckled, and took their plates to the sink. "That's a good one. We better get out and get the stuff for the babies and some groceries for you before the storm breaks. I want to watch every bit of it."

"I don't believe you talked me into buying a baby blanket. Look at those fat cats. Asleep like never before."

He rinsed out the bottles they had bought and joined her at the door.

The first drops of rain were pelting the deck. She was watching the storm, and all the while she was thinking about him and how so very gentle he was as they had fed the tiny kittens their milk. His square hands had held them so surely and carefully. And she had caught him smiling the first time one of them caught onto the bottle and started nursing hungrily.

They had put the kittens to bed, snuggled in the folds of the cotton blanket with blue and yellow ducks on it. She had left him to put the rest of the groceries away. He had complained when she had piled the shopping cart with ice cream, pizza, hot dogs, Fritos, and burgers. He had just stood patiently waiting while she added french fries and Crisco. His only contribution had been popcorn.

The wind and the ripping water had calmed just a little. The rain increased to a blinding downpour. He stood beside her a moment. His voice was low and menacing. "I came here to be alone and now I have a neighbor and three cats."

Declining the urge to look at him, Sterling smiled at the storm. "Life's full of surprises, Joe. How about that poker game? Can't see much anymore. Fog setting in."

"Don't feel like cards," he grunted. "Let's play Jeopardy."

She turned and looked at him questioningly. He answered

with a forced smile. "Like you're in jeopardy if you don't give me some straight answers."

"Are you going to grill me? Isn't that cop lingo?" She chuckled and then, realizing he was dead serious again, stopped. "Look, Joe, don't start again. I'm just me. And you're just you. We'll talk if you like, converse. But not just about me."

They moved to the couch, and she followed his example by propping her feet on the coffee table for comfort. He looked toward the ceiling. "Why me? Why does this woman come to the ocean and pick me out to bother. She jabbers incessantly, she just pushes her way in here and takes over. I'm a cop. A tough guy. And she's riding roughshod over me. Why?"

"Maybe you ticked Him off," she chided, joining in the spirit. "Not a good thing to do." Kicking off her shoes, Sterling curled up on the couch. "I could do with a good fire right now. Why don't you have any wood in here?"

The ability of her mind to jump from one thing to another so quickly amused him. After considering her question, he answered. "Didn't come with the place. Whatever didn't come, I don't have. Besides, it's usually hot and humid. What the hell would I do with firewood?"

"There's some at my place. If this keeps up till tonight, we'll go over there, heat a pizza, and watch *Casablanca*. Sound good?"

"No."

"No?" She pretended to be hurt.

He stretched his tired body. "You go over there and watch whatever. I'll stay here and have some peace."

Because the shadows beneath his eyes were darker and his patience getting thinner, she asked, "You didn't sleep last night. Why?"

He was resting his head on the back of the couch. He turned to look at her. "I don't sleep most nights. And you know why."

"You have to get past that, Joe."

His voice held an edge as he tested his tolerance. "Yeah. Tell me how, Miss Know-it-all."

"You can't punish yourself for the rest of your life. You have to let it go. You must know that." She was being pushy. It was her job.

He was silent for a few minutes, obviously mulling something over and over in his mind. Without turning to her he said, "I keep seeing his face while he was dying. It only took five maybe ten seconds after I got to him. He was surprised." Joe went to the refrigerator and put ice in a glass. It was only noon but he was mixing a martini. She winced when he plopped two fat olives into his drink. She didn't speak for fear that he wouldn't continue.

Returning, he stared into space as he took a gulp of the drink. "He was damn surprised. He knew it was my bullet that hit him. It was dark. Pitch black. We recognized each other at the same instant . . ." His voice was flat. He was looking away from her now and she watched as his fingers tightened around the glass. Holding her breath, Sterling waited for his grip to shatter it right in his hand.

"But I had already pressed off," he continued, as if to himself. "There was no way to stop the bullet. No way."

She heard the strain in his voice. Sensed the pain that gripped his body . . . squeezed his very soul. She felt a chill creep along her spine and raise the hair at her neck. She wanted to reach over and touch his arm. She wanted to cradle him and make him forget, just for a moment. No human being should suffer like this.

"He grabbed hold of my jacket," he began again. "I tried to keep him from falling, but we both fell, slowly at first and then we were on the sidewalk. His blood was all over my hands." He held his hand in front of him and flexed it a few times, watching it. And then as if he had just come out of a dark tunnel, he turned toward her and smiled. "Ever walked in the rain?"

She was instantly alert. It hadn't been a normal transition. Thought processes just didn't swing that suddenly. She felt a tingle of fear. Was he losing it? "Not lately. A warm rain, maybe, but not that cold downpour."

He put his shoes on. "You've been calling all the shots so far, lady. I say we walk in the cold rain." He took her hand and pulled her to her feet.

"No," she protested, realizing he was serious.

"Yes, wrap up. It's a good experience. Put your shoes on." He had to get out of here, had to redirect his thinking.

"No. We'll catch cold." She tried to tug her hand free.

"So what? Put your shoes on or I'll carry you out there."

She pulled her shoes on and headed for the door. "At least let me get my jacket." She stretched her free hand toward her flannel shirt that lay over the back of a chair and grabbed it on the way out.

He still had her by the hand and was pulling her out onto the rain-slick deck. The rain was cold and had slowed somewhat. She wrapped her free arm around herself and looked at him. Was he crazy?

He pulled her down the steps behind him and then they jogged hand in hand. She felt her own anger rising. They would both get sick. "Joe."

"Run." Ignoring her protests, he increased the pace until they were both puffing.

She jerked her hand free of his and stopped. He slid and whirled around. "What's the matter? In a situation you can't control?" He mocked her. "Oh, just a minor one, but not in control one little bit. Don't like it, do you? Well, multiply that feeling times a hundred, a thousand, and then maybe, just maybe, you'll get an idea of how I feel."

They were both drenched and cold. His hair was plastered against his head and rain ran in rivulets down his face. His eyes were pain-filled and proud. His mouth was caught in a grim line. His nostrils flared with each breath.

He pinned her with his eyes, and she returned his stare, chin tilted. Without a word, she turned back in the direction they'd been running and began again.

"What the hell are you doing?" he yelled after her, perplexed.

"Getting used to it," she hollered back and continued. "Maybe you better try taking some of your own medicine." Her shoes were soggy. It was getting difficult to pick one up after the other. The sand was mushy and made the going even rougher. She wondered to herself if she had any idea what she was doing. This was stupid. This was a job much too big for her. He needed help and she didn't know if she was qualified to give it.

She was caught in his strong arms and slammed to the ground. He fell halfway across her. Sterling took the solid weight of him and searched for his face in the rain.

"You're some crazy lady." The wet warmth of his body seared her as he lowered his face to hers. His breath whispered across her ear. It felt good, so good, but she wouldn't let him know it. Gathering some strength, she rolled and pinned him beneath her. Looking down at him, at the surprise on his face, she had to smile.

"Had enough, tough guy?" she challenged him with a wide grin.

His hands came up and he molded his fingers to her face. Slowly, he ran his thumbs across her cheeks, her lips. What she saw in his eyes right then might have been the Joe before all this happened. "Not nearly," he whispered before he pulled her mouth to his.

His lips were wet and cool, but they soon warmed under hers as they moved from one corner of her mouth to the other. She felt the sand stick to her hands as she traced his shoulders. She could feel the strength there, the solidness. She felt the cold rain rolling down her back, but she had no inclination to move. This sensation, this wandering heat that his body drew from hers, was demanding on its own. His kiss was gentle but unrelenting and she moved her body more in line with his as he slipped his tongue into her mouth.

A need, a desire that Sterling didn't know she possessed rose to the surface and cried for more. His gentleness was fast turning into urgency, his soft mouth was no longer asking, but taking. And she gave and took and gave some more. His hands slipped under her shirt and found her. He rolled then, turning her beneath him. When the rain hit her full in the face again, reality came with it.

"Joe."

He reared his head back and looked at her. Water ran from his face onto hers, but she could see the blatant desire in his eyes, then the steely control that flicked into them. He was on his feet pulling her up behind him. Without a word, he led her back to the cottage, up the stairs, across the deck, and into the living room. He left her standing near the doors and went into the bathroom.

He returned with two gigantic fluffy towels. He draped one over her shoulders and dropped the other to the floor. He undid the buttons of her shirt and pushed it back toward her shoulders. His eyes never left hers. They were dark and foreboding. She felt a chill from fear, not the cold. He ran his hands over the towel, absorbing water from her body. She wanted to lean into him. She wanted to shove logic from her mind and let her body and her heart rule. But somehow it almost seemed as if he were trying to vent his frustrations on her. It almost felt like he needed to hurt someone the way he'd been hurt, and she couldn't let it be that way. She dragged air through her lungs and leveled her gaze on his dark and sleepy eyes. She put her hands on his wrists to stop him. "Joe, I don't . . . I . . . it's too fast. We don't . . ."

He stopped. Restraint seemed foreign to him. It seemed to Sterling that he was fighting his own nature. "You do something to me, Sterling. You touch me where I haven't been touched in a long time, and sometimes I forget that we're strangers. Go home, lady, and stay there. Next time I might not stop."

She wanted to be in his embrace, didn't she? She didn't want to even think of going back to her cottage alone. But if she held him, if she comforted him . . . Was that what she was doing?

No. Her body cried out for his, wanted his. What had gone wrong with the reason why she was here? All of a sudden she wanted to call Mr. Ramsburg and tell him that all Joe Timothy MacDaniels needed was Sterling Powell. That was foolish. She redid the buttons as he turned his back to her and looked out across the ocean. The muscles in his back rippled beneath his wet shirt. Wanting to comfort couldn't be the reason for this.

Could it be she was falling in love with a man she barely knew? Could she be misconstruing all of this with her innate need to help her fellow human beings. If making love was what this man needed could she . . . No, it couldn't be any of those things. She picked the towel up off the floor and draped it over his shoulders, rubbing to chase the chill from him. Sand dusted to the floor.

He whirled on her and threw the towel across the room. "Damn it, woman, get away from me now before I never let you leave this house again."

She jumped back from the wave of fury. Until now none of his real anger had been directed at her. She didn't like it. She was afraid of him and yet she wanted to touch him all at the same time. She made a mad dash past him and sprinted toward her own cottage. The rain hid the tears. She was glad because the last thing he needed to see was that he had affected her so deeply.

She tossed her wet clothes on the floor and filled the bathtub with bubbles and water so hot that she could barely get in it. She tried to relax her tense muscles. Squeezing her eyes shut, she tried to block out the images in her mind. Her assignments had never been this confusing.

Of course, she had to be realistic. She was dealing with a much more difficult situation than usual. Perhaps she should just go and leave him alone. Later might be a better time to assess his needs. *His* needs? What about *her* needs? She added more hot water and slid down in the tub till her chin touched the water.

He was a complex man. His emotions ran strong and deep. Joe was at war with himself and therefore the whole world. What would it be like? She could only guess what he was feeling. She would want to return to the womb. Curl up and go away, out of the world forever. Did men react the same way? She doubted it.

He wanted to kill again. She could see it in his eyes, in the way he moved. Maybe kindness wasn't what he needed. Maybe he needed to be yelled at and bullied. Maybe he required a good shake. He wanted the memories of what he did to die. That's what he wanted to kill. What he had done.

She dried herself off and left the bathroom. Walking naked into the hall, she made a right turn toward her bedroom. It was then she saw him. Sitting on the couch, watching her.

"Get dressed, Powell. We're going to drive up the coast till we reach sunshine, and then we're going to a movie and dinner." He wasn't smiling. He was fresh from a shower himself; she could smell his spicy aftershave. Jekyll and Hyde? How could a man swing from one mood to the other so quickly?

"You're going to catch cold." He nodded toward her nakedness and she scampered into her room.

Sterling dressed in front of the mirror, noticing her cheeks were flushed. She hadn't blushed since she was sixteen. She was beginning to think she had been jettisoned into the twilight zone. Things were not making sense at all.

Her aqua-blue skirt was set off with a shocking pink sash. Her hair always curled unruly when she didn't dry it right away, falling this way and that over her shoulders. Shaking it, she drew herself up. Giving herself one last glimpse in the mirror, she took a deep breath and reminded herself she was getting paid handsomely for this job. She'd make a good one of it.

He stood up when she walked into the room. He had on stonewashed denims and cowboy boots. He wore a white shirt, with the cuffs rolled up to the elbows. His forearms were roped with muscles and tanned. She admired his wrists and hands. He had the hands of an artist, small-boned at the wrist, then widening out at the palm, and fingers that were blunt and competent. She pictured them wrapped around a gun.

"I'm not going to say I'm sorry about what happened. I'm not in control of things anymore. That's why I isolated myself out here. I'd like to make it up to you even though you brought on most of it yourself."

She nodded. He was right. "No apology accepted because none is needed. And you're on, but we'll take my car this time."

"What, now something's wrong with the way I drive?" he growled.

She laughed as he followed her outside. "It's simply my turn, cop. No big deal. Nothing sinister behind it. It's just my turn. Okay?"

She stopped beside the rental that had been dropped off last night and raised an eyebrow at him, waiting for an answer.

"Okay. You drive." Then he saw the sharp little black Porsche. "Do you have a fairy godmother?"

"Sort of," she said slyly, and got into the car when he opened the door for her. She slipped the key in the ignition and had the 944 in motion before he was fully seated.

Sterling pulled away from the small ocean town and stomped on the gas pedal. "Sunshine, here we come."

He covered his face and groaned. "The roads are wet."

"Don't be a cop today, MacDaniels."

FOUR

Kicking in the turbo, Sterling glanced at Joe only to see him turn disbelieving eyes on her.

She shrugged. "I just wanted you to see what it would do. Relax, I won't get us killed." *Good line, Sterling*, she said to herself as he turned to glance out the side window. Hurriedly, she added, "How far is sunshine? Any idea?" She let the car coast down to fifty-five miles per hour.

"When you see yellow instead of gray, I'd bet that was it. Do you always drive like you talk, fast and nonstop?" He'd never met anyone like this lady. Whoever was trying to do a job on him had picked a real challenge. Of course, what better way to keep him off guard. Send a beautiful, flighty, airheaded woman to live next to him and torture him into talking. And about what? He had no reason to kill Red. Red was his friend. It was more than that. It was probably pressure from the department to clean up what was a dubious operation to begin with. He knew that.

"Don't be quiet, Joe. Sometimes too much thinking is worse than none."

He looked back at her and stated flatly, "You must be one superior secretary to receive a salary that supports this car."

"I am," she thought fast, "executive secretary to the president of," she hoped he missed the slight falter in her voice as she conjured up a name, "Preston Industries. Surely you've heard of it. Offices all over the world. Computers. Oil. Gas." She shrugged. "You name it and we're into it." Telling the lie made her squirm a little in the seat. Some things were necessary. She'd set them right later.

He cranked the window to vent the smoke as he lit the long brown cigarello. Examining the finery inside the car, he stretched his legs and tried to relax.

The road unfolded before them, flat and unending. Sand, grass, short and tall, tasseled and bent, lined the asphalt. The ocean veered away from them as they continued up the coast.

Sterling turned on the radio. A jumpy light rock tune filled the air and she turned the volume up full. Tapping her fingers on the steering wheel and singing along, she felt his gaze on her just before he reached to turn the radio down to a whisper.

"You always try to put holes in your eardrums? I don't understand it. People complain about excess noise on the job, kids playing too loudly, jets flying too low, and scaring Grandpa's cows and then they get in their cars and blast themselves deaf."

She merely smiled and flashed a glance at him. "You have to have it loud to feel it."

"No, you really don't." He flipped the dial until he picked up a station that played classical music. "Now just listen to this . . . don't be vibrated by it."

The mood instantly changed inside the close quarters of

the car. As the intimate sounds of a piano backed by violins filled the air, Sterling felt herself tensing.

She flipped her hair off her shoulder. "Richard Clayderman."

His look was one of surprise, his voice sarcastic. "So you're not totally unfamiliar with good music."

Sterling ignored his comment and smiled to herself smugly, braking as the traffic in front of her slowed. It was still raining, but the sky was getting lighter.

"Not totally," she agreed evenly. "But there's nothing wrong with a good old country song, and some of the light rock is okay. I'm pretty partial to the oldies, but I like music, all kinds."

He nodded and tried to listen to the music. "At one time I found great pleasure in all types of music. Even wrote some pretty good songs." He let the pleasure of the memories roll through him.

"Didn't sing too badly, either. Me and Red, we used to sit on the porch of his hunting cabin up in Cumberland and pick and strum." He remembered too well. His voice softened. "We'd throw back a few beers and make up silly lyrics." But now the music was just a sound. It didn't touch him. It couldn't reach him where he was now. He hated it.

When he rolled the window back up, he caught her scent. It was light and flowery. He wished his biological responses had become as deadened as his heart and soul.

"Traffic is getting thicker. Guess we're getting close to a town. Want to stop here or go on?"

Without looking her way, he stated flatly, "Keep going. The whole point of this was to reach sunshine. Do you see any?"

I keep getting to him, she thought. *But irritation is better than no emotion. It might be only a little tiny bit at a time, but I'm getting there.* "Surliness will only get you turned around. I refuse to drive any more than another half hour. Whatever is there at . . ." she glanced at the clock on the dash, "four o'clock is where we stop."

"Now that makes a lot of sense. I can see why your boss sent you away for a while. You must drive everybody crazy." He watched the passing landscape as they drove. Once upon a time he would have enjoyed the view. But no pleasure came.

Was it her imagination or was he trying to press himself against the door to keep a good distance between them? No matter, she shrugged mentally. Distance was one thing she didn't plan on giving him.

"What are you watching in the rearview mirror?" he questioned sourly. "It's where we're going that you're supposed to be watching."

"That one stupid car changes lanes when I do and speeds up or slows down along with me. Strange."

"The car can't be stupid," he said drolly, "but the driver might be. And what's so strange about it? We're driving along the same stretch of road."

At 3:55 they followed the road into a small village. She could smell the sea air immediately and broke into a wide grin. The houses lining the road into town were small cottages with picket fences, swings in the backyard and on the porches. Toys were scattered all over the yards along with scooters and bikes.

Turning right onto Main Street, Sterling said gleefully, "All right! Quaint, by the sea . . . Look down there. Masts, the tall ships and real fishermen. A real by-gosh fishing village. We'll stop here."

He grumbled, "No sun and it's not four o'clock. Keep driving."

"Sun will be out soon, and if I slow down and take my time parking it will be precisely four. This is the place. Oh, look, shops. I love to shop."

"How come I knew that? And I suppose you're hungry already, too."

She pulled the sleek automobile into a parking space and turned the ignition off. "I could do with some seafood, shrimp deep fried and dripping with tartar sauce, or buttered lobster, white, sleek, and greasy. And curly fries. I wonder if curly fries have hit the outer banks yet?"

They both slipped out of their seat belts and got out of the car. The air just burst with the smell of salt and fish. He put his forearms on the roof of the car and looked at her. "Ever heard of natural-grain bread and vegetables . . . the green ones that are good for you."

"Ooooh." She made a face at him and slammed the car door. "Sea kelp and green beans. Not on your life. You can have whatever you like. I'm not opposed to watching someone eat that stuff. Come on, MacDaniels. Let's look this town over. I'm sure I can find something to spend money on. There's got to be a few touristy shops mixed in with the basic ones."

They walked close to each other from the parking lot to the sidewalks of the street. It was fairly quiet. A few visitors milled here and there, cameras hanging around their necks. Locals went about their business of putting dimes in parking meters, unloading delivery trucks, and pumping gas in their cars. An older man sat on a rickety wooden chair in front of the gas station doing absolutely nothing but looking around. Sterling threw her hand up to him and he responded with a nod and a weary smile.

Joe decided it might be a good time to coax some information out of her. The direct approach of demanding to know her game hadn't worked so he would try a different way. "New York is certainly a different world than this. That old man sitting in front of the gas station could be arrested for loitering."

"You ought to know. I don't suppose D.C. is much different. I'll bet you were a fair but firm cop. Am I right?"

She did it again, changed the direction of the conversation. He put his hands in his pockets to stifle the urge to throttle her. "I was good at my job."

"Do you miss it?" she asked innocently as she paused to look in the window of a curio shop.

"I don't miss anything." He looked away from the shop toward the docks.

"Really?" She looked at him and reminded herself to be patient—and patiently goad him. "Must be nice to be able to simply cut yourself off from everything that meant something to you."

"Some things you have no control over."

She turned her most innocent face to him. "Name one."

He pretended interest in the shop window now, simply to avoid her eyes. "I merely said I didn't miss anything. It didn't call for a lengthy discussion."

Sterling looked at his reflection in the window. *Yeah,* she thought, *yes you do. You miss everything.*

"Look at that castle," she cried delightedly. "Isn't it beautiful? Look at all those little steps. They're cut so precisely." She moved to get a better look and squealed again. "When you move around, it winks and sparkles with a rainbow of colors. Emerald. The emerald castle. It makes me really believe in the impossible. It sets my imagination fleeing up the steps and into the arms of my Prince Charming. I love it."

She scooted around Joe and into the store. She flashed him an excited grin. He watched her bounce to the young sales clerk and practically drag her over to the three-inch-high piece of cut crystal to inquire about the price. The clerk turned it up and showed Sterling the price tag. A frown creased her forehead and then her face fell in disappointment. She thought for only a second before she shook her head and thanked the woman.

She walked back to join Joe and took one more longing look at the piece of glass, and then the frown was gone and replaced with a shine of expectation of what the next shop might offer.

"You can afford a Porsche but not a chunk of glass?" He fell in step beside her. Her shoulder brushed his.

"Eighty dollars? It's wonderful and magical and plays with my mind, but I am sensible most of the time. Now here's a good place. Probably nothing over fifty-nine cents." She grabbed his hand and pulled him in behind her, but he didn't miss the second wistful glance she threw back toward her castle.

It was a real tourist junk shop. Straw hats hung from the ceiling. Plastic sea gulls flew from fishwire between them. Racks on the wall held T-shirts and shorts, sweatshirts and bandanas. Counters ran through the middle of the store filled with gaudy shell art and jewelry. Ashtrays with questionable sayings and toilet paper that played music stood alongside glasses advertising Delaware. He felt out of place and foolish. He wondered for the third time what he was doing here and why he was with this woman. To find out what her reason for being in North Ocean City was, he reminded himself as he picked up an ashtray with a sea gull perched on a pier stuck on it. He set it back down with a decided klunk.

Sterling chattered to everyone. It didn't seem to matter if they worked there or not, she managed to find something to say to all of them. She ran back to him and tugged on his jacket sleeve.

"You have got to see these earrings."

He reluctantly followed her to the jewelry case and looked from her to the earrings and back again. "They're awful."

"I know," she said delightedly and turned to the sales clerk. "I'll take them, and don't put them in a bag, I'm going to wear them."

Sterling attached the sea shells with trailing silver chains to her ears as they left the shop. They swung as she walked and tangled in her hair.

"Oh, I forgot my hat. The big straw one. I bought that, too." She turned and dashed back in the store and came out adorned in a really badly worked straw sombrero.

"It's tacky and they're terrible. You look silly . . ." he stated, all the while fighting back a smile. He wanted to laugh, but he figured that was what she wanted, and he wouldn't do it. Either she was an extremely clever woman or she was simply recovering from a frontal lobotomy.

"I know, isn't it wonderful?" she rattled on. "Now here's serious stuff. Let's go look at the ten-carat diamonds and rubies. I love gold. Just the feel of it. Let's go. I always thought it would be so neat to be in a big fancy restaurant and sit under those lights that make all your jewelry sparkle and catch people in the eye. Rings on every finger." She held her hand in front of her and elegantly wiggled her fingers.

She was bouncing rather than walking as they went into the jewelry store. A little bell over the door jangled and two heads turned their way to smile a greeting.

They were the only people in the shop. The obvious proprietors were in their sixties, at least. Both had gray hair, old, tired bodies, and gleaming eyes. They exchanged a knowing, sweet look as they watched the young couple walk around looking in the cases.

Sterling didn't miss that glance and it plucked at something hidden deep away inside her. A quick assessment of the couple told Sterling that they had been together a long time. They had seen a lot of things in their lifetime, tragedies and comedies, and they had held fast to each other and they had made it . . . happily.

She sighed as she admired the pretty gems. She and Jerry could have eventually been like the proprietors. She briefly wondered what things would be like now if she had gone out onto the tarmack and simply stopped him from going—

Joe's voice broke into her thoughts. "From the looks

of you, these people have to know you're not going to buy anything. Why take up their time?''

"You are such a grouch, Joe. Relax. People browse all the time." She stopped long enough to look up at him. "Are you just naturally surly?"

"And if I am, it's my business. Get on with it," he grunted and turned to another display case and pretended to examine the gold and silver all lined up in neat, expensive rows.

Sterling caught the owners watching them and smiling. Young lovers. Is that what they looked like to the world? Would it be such a ridiculous thing?

"Good afternoon." She directed her thoughts and herself to the people behind the counter. "I'd like to buy a silver charm for my six-year-old niece. She's just started to take dancing lessons. A ballerina. Could I see what you have?"

Joe moved over to the door, leaned against the jamb and just watched her. She was so lit up. How could she be so happy all the time? *Why* was she so happy all the time? What was that small momentary lapse when they had first entered the shop as she had sighed and a fleeting sadness had darted across her face? It had vanished almost as soon as it appeared . . . What had triggered it?

The purchase made, along with new friends, they left the store twenty minutes later.

The next shop was a women's boutique. He stopped when she tugged him by the hand again. "Not this time. I'll just wander around out here for a little while."

"Wimp. I think God should have given men the glee it takes to shop. Women would be much happier. You're not having a good time."

"I said we'd go. I didn't say I'd enjoy myself."

Oh, well. She was getting him out, circulating his blood, and stimulating the gray matter. Let him sulk if he must. She disappeared into the store between the circular racks of clothing, sporting all colors and sizes.

They were only half a block down from the docks. Joe could see the ocean and hear the sway and bump of ships tied to the docks. He had always loved the sea. He guessed that was why he headed down this way. He did find some kind of peace with it, but he knew he couldn't accept the solace. So he fought it. It was the same with the tugging that went on inside him when he was with this woman. War. Always war of one kind or another. All he wanted was . . . He shrugged.

A horn blew close by. Kids rode two-wheelers down the street. A kite bounced in the sky, skittering on the changing breezes. A dog wandered up to him, took one look at him, and wandered on his way. Joe found he had been on the verge of bending down to ruffle the dog's fur when the animal decided he didn't look friendly.

Peace. He rolled the word over in his mind. Was that what he wanted? The guilt, the sadness, the total shock of what he had done still overwhelmed him so much that thinking was hard. It was hard to sequence things. It was hard to concentrate and, sometimes when he did, the scenes he played over in his mind only served to tear him up even more. He knew all about physical pain. Emotional and mental pain were also no strangers. This was such a totally different thing . . . He couldn't even think of a word for it. It was easier to be mad, angry with the whole world and everyone in it. It was easier to be mindlessly depressed than to think.

When Sterling whirled out of the shop, Joe laughed heartily, involuntarily, and shook his head.

She was dressed in an off-the-shoulder bright-yellow blouse and a below-the-knee Gypsy skirt that sported every color in the rainbow. In a bag, dangling from her hand, were her clothes and her shoes. She turned around twice so the skirt swirled around her knees. "Well, what do you think?"

"I think you're crazy as hell." But he didn't miss the smooth nearly tanned swell of her breasts just where the blouse rested. He didn't miss the curving sleekness of legs as the skirt settled. And he couldn't miss the delight in her pretty eyes or not want to catch her smiling mouth with his. He only had time to wonder how all this was happening to him, through the haze of despair, when she caught her arm through his and led him to the little restaurant.

"I see picnic tables down by the docks. We'll get carry-out and sit down there. What do you say?" She looked up at him with a warmth that touched him.

"Don't you want to find a nice expensive restaurant that can serve you up that dripping lobster?"

"Not especially. Maybe another time. I'd like to sit at the tables and watch the world go by."

"The sun's out," he said as he squinted upward. "I guess if you promise the sun will shine and it does, I should trust your decision to eat at the picnic tables."

She casually hugged his arm to her as they went inside. He bent close to her ear and asked, "Aren't you embarrassed to look this ridiculous?"

"No." She strolled up to the counter. "You do have carry-out, right? Good," she nodded at the young man with the paper cap on his head and scanned the menu on the board above the stove, "I'll have two hot dogs with ketchup and onions. No make that onion rings and french fries. Do you have the curly ones?"

"No, ma'am," the boy said as he looked at Joe for help.

Joe simply stood by silently and watched nonchalantly as the hapless creation of color and sound rambled on. When it was his turn he ordered two slices of pizza with black olives and pepperoni and two long necks.

A little boy burst through the door of the restaurant, closely followed by his fussing mother. The child ran toward the counter, lickety split, and bumped smack into Sterling, propelling him backward and down to the floor with a thud.

Without so much as a moment's hesitation, the handsome little fellow jumped right back up, but Sterling knew he must have whacked his elbow pretty hard on the floor. She bent and picked him up, cradling him on her hip. "Whoa there, cowboy. Slow down. You'll tire your horse out before the day is over."

The knowledge was immediate. It was a mistake. But one she couldn't recognize until it was too late. It had simply been a natural reaction. Anyone would have done it. The wave of déjà vu hit her hard.

It was so natural to have the boy in her arms. His face was gooey from the lollipop he managed not to drop through all this and he was smiling up at her with a cupid's-bow mouth and bright, eager eyes. Memories flooded back. Pictures of her own child wavered before her eyes. A wave of pain washed over her again and again, so powerful that she reeled with it. She felt the hot sting of tears as they tried to force their way out and she squeezed her eyes shut tight for an instant.

Blocking the memories as they seared painfully across her heart, Sterling took one more look at the baby hand that rested at her breast and then she set him down on his wiggly little feet and patted his head. She couldn't control it much longer. She had to get out of there. This had never happened before and she didn't know how to handle it.

The child's mother took the toddler's hand. "I'm sorry, miss. He just runs everywhere he goes. I wonder how I'll ever keep up with him."

"It's all right," she said, surprised that her voice sounded quite calm and normal. Sterling crouched down until she was eye level with the little boy. "Children have a way of rambling fearlessly through life." His hair was so fine and soft. Her son's hair had been that way. There were chocolate stains on his shirt from an earlier treat.

"How many do you have?" the mother asked as she

pried the lollipop from his hand. "It's got dirt on it, Petey."

"None," Sterling answered, standing up and feeling the razor cut of her own words. "Take good care of your mom.

"Joe," Sterling turned her attention to him and said as brightly as she could, "would you wait for our order? I'll find us the best picnic table out there."

Without waiting for his answer, Sterling was out the door and out of sight. Joe looked from her to the head of the small boy. What was that all about? He looked toward the door that Sterling had bolted through. That lady is so intense. Either intensely happy or intensely silly or intensely stubborn. Or intensely hurt. What was that he had seen on her face? His concern made him impatient with the blundering efforts of the young clerk behind the counter.

Outside, Sterling jogged to the edge of the dock and swiped at big, round tears that ran down her cheeks. Grabbing a tissue out of her purse, she dried them and swore at herself, only to feel fresh ones course down her cheeks. Forcing deep breaths, offering her face to the wind off the sea, she managed to look nearly presentable. But inside, the ache wouldn't let up. It made her angry.

She found the table closest to the water and wiped the seats down with the shirt she had worn. She looked out to sea for diversion and found Timmy's face wouldn't fade from her mind. Her son. He would have been almost nine now. Holding the boy in the restaurant had brought back the feelings of how good it had been to hold him in her arms, feel his little hands grab on to her . . . She missed it so.

"That's the slickest way I've seen yet to get out of paying your bill. Are you all right?" Joe's concerned voice came from behind her.

From years of practice, Sterling pasted a shallow smile on her face. She nodded, taking the bags from his hand,

and helped him place the food on the tables and dispense with the wrappers. Because of the breeze, everything wanted to slide off the surface, so she weighed everything down with the contents and watched as Joe swung a leg over the bench opposite her and examined her suspiciously.

It was the first really acceptable thing she had seen in his eyes besides amusement. In the sunlight, his eyes appeared almost green. She was somehow comforted by what she saw there. Soulmates. Comrades in pain. She wasn't ready to share hers with him. Not yet.

"Of course I am. That little kid could have cracked his elbow a good one, that's all." She pushed the hot dog down further in the bun and licked ketchup off her finger.

Watching her carefully, he unwrapped his pizza. "It was more than that and you know it. Tell me about it."

"Why don't you just eat, Joe," she clipped and took at bite of the hot dog. It was tasteless. She was disappointed in herself. The meal was spoiled.

He didn't like being dismissed, so he persisted gently. "Because I want to know what caused that kid to affect you that way. I don't really know anything about you, Sterling. So enlighten me."

Although she tried to be civil, she snapped, "It's really none of your business." Then softening her voice and her attitude she scolded herself for her harshness. There wasn't any sense taking out her anger on him. "I'm fine. Look, the sun is bright now and, oh, look at those boats. Fishing must be a hard way to make a living. I'm glad to see that people still do it the old way. A hard day's work for a day's pay, then home to the little woman to see if she has a pot of stew on the stove."

Did she really think he could be so easily diverted? There was a silence. A stiff one. He watched her. Tried to figure out what had knocked the bounce from her. The pizza in his hand felt cold. He put it back down. For now he would let her get away without answering his question. But not without comment.

Joe pulled a key chain from his pocket and popped the tops from the two bottles of long-neck beer. "It's okay for you to poke your nose into my business but I better not do the same to you, right?" He set one of the bottles in front of her.

"Thank you." She put the beer to her lips and turned it up for a bracing swallow. When she replaced the bottle back on the table her hand was instantly wet with foam as the liquid spewed up and into the air.

Joe laughed at her amazed glare. He stopped at her look. "I can see you don't know how to drink a long neck." He chuckled as he wiped splashes of beer from her hand with a napkin. She looked at his hand working over hers, felt the gentleness in his touch, and had to smile up at him.

"You're going to tell me there's some dumb secret to drinking out of a beer bottle?" She pulled the bottle closer and looked into it.

"A long neck, yes. You sip it and set the bottle down slowly. Or you get drenched."

"That's stupid." She pushed the bottle away from her.

"That's real life." He grinned, because she was off guard and she was perplexed. And she looked so beautifully ridiculous in that get-up. He laughed because it was there and it felt good and because, somehow, it seemed to make her feel better.

"I want a Coke," she stated flatly.

FIVE

He folded his pizza and took a bite. "This is rubbery and cold," he announced.

"It's supposed to be. Don't you do anything but gripe?" She tried to sound light and interested. He was beginning to loosen up even if it was reluctantly. And that was her job, wasn't it? She had pried the lid from his coffin and managed to get him out of it for a while. But how long would it last? How long could it last?

Here she was feeling sorry for herself and yet she was supposed to be helping him. Sometimes, such as in moments like this one, she wished there was someone for her to lean on. Just for a while. She had kept herself busy. Kept interested in helping other people. It had worked for these past five years and then pow—it came to her out of the blue wearing tiny Adidas shoes and little denim overalls. Until moments like now, she didn't allow herself the time to think about how much she missed the evenings when Timmy would go to sleep at a reasonable hour and she and Jerry would curl up together in front of the fireplace. It was so easy to recall the safe, protected, loved feeling. God, she missed it all so much.

He watched her. She was concentrating too much on the food. In the short time they had known each other he had filed one piece of information on her. She enjoyed eating, loved it. . . .

Something was on her mind. Something she wasn't willing to share just yet. "Sterling is a strange name. How'd you come by it?" He reached over and wiped ketchup from her chin with the beer-soaked napkin.

Grateful for the diversion from her own thoughts, Sterling grimaced. "My mother loved fine things. Art, porcelain, silver."

He grinned a little just to cheer her up. "Could have named you Brass then, couldn't she?" He hadn't cared much for her when she was all wound up and he cared even less for the fact that now she seemed torn up by something. It did something to his gut.

The floodlight-across-the-dark-parking-lot smile of hers played on her face. He had to admit it. He liked her. Even above the purely male interest, he liked the flaky broad. But he still had to find out what she was up to and put a stop to it.

Sterling studied Joe. The little bit of gray in his hair was visible in the direct sunlight. He was a handsome man. Her Jerry had been handsome, too. He hadn't had a mustache, but he *had* had long sideburns and his hair had been unruly, like Joe's. She could almost remember the way it felt to kiss him. She lowered her lashes to keep the memory to herself.

"Where were you born?" His question surprised her. So far he had shown no interest in such personal details.

"Oklahoma. Tulsa, to be more exact. I love that place. My folks are schoolteachers. Elementary school and high school. So you can guess how they were always too involved in my life in or out of school. But I developed a talent for entertaining myself early and taking care of myself.'' The breeze pushed her hair across her face and Sterling shoved it back with the back of her hand. She realized what he was doing. Changing the subject. Getting her mind on other things. Just as she had been doing to him all along. Okay, she admitted to herself, so it was a relief to think of something else.

"How did you like growing up in Indiana?" she asked.

Sterling saw the flash of suspicion on his face and squelched it just as quickly by qualifying her information. "The newspaper was very thorough."

"We were farmers," he said after a moment's pause. "I went to school just enough to satisfy everyone. The rest of the days I went hunting and fishing. Never knew anything about game seasons. Anyone saw me they just shrugged and said, 'There goes that MacDaniels kid again.' I enjoyed it."

"And you never had any trouble with grades?"

His brows drew together as he cocked his head to study her questioningly. "Why get A's if C's are passing?"

She shrugged and finished a french fry. "That's one way to think about it. You're a smart man. A road scholar?"

"What makes you say that?" He swung his leg over the bench so he was sitting with his side to her, one elbow leaning on the table. "Well?"

"The way you move, the way you absorb everything. The way you assess anything that comes your way. You know a lot about a lot of things. You catalogue information and file it away in your brain. Besides that, you have made a success of your career."

He didn't deny it. He did exactly that. He had a good memory and was proud of it. You needed it to get the job done. He didn't comment on it. There was no reason to.

Sterling watched Joe. He was a much more passionate man than Jerry had been. Jerry had been easygoing and laid back. Joe was energetic. Filled with a force that drove him. "Vietnam. It must have been very difficult to be there?" she asked nonchalantly.

She didn't miss the flicker of suspicion in his eyes. "It was no Sunday school picnic." Not by a long shot. "I was Fire Team leader for an infantry rifle squad, 5th Mech. Da Krong Valley, Gio Lihn, Con Thien. We were headquartered at Quang Tri. Why did you bring that up?" He squinted in the waning sunlight.

"Just making conversation. I care about the veterans. I'm proud to know someone who was there. I'm glad we have you guys to take care of things, keep us safe. You couldn't have gotten much farther north could you? Were you drafted?"

"I enlisted. Three years. The last year I got my orders to go in country. Corporal J.T. MacDaniels. I haven't thought about him in a while." And he hadn't. "How did you know I was there?" *The nightmares,* he thought grimly, *were of a different sort now.*

"I read about it. What can I say? I subscribe to many newspapers. Didn't you read any of the accounts of the accident?"

"Sure, I'd want to read all about it. Did it have nice gory pictures, too?" He balled up his trash and pitched it into the can. Turning up his beer, he took a long swallow and then eyed her tenuously. "Tell me who you are, Sterling. Just spit it out and we can simply get on with it. I can tell you to get lost and you can go back and tell whoever sent you here that it's a no-go."

"It's all so simple for you, isn't it? I feel like I've known you for years. Yesterday I might have considered leaving here, but not now. Why can't we just be friends and do our thing? I need a rest, and even though you're not the most willing neighbor or companion, I have sort of gotten used to you." That was a lie. She would never get used to or be complacent with him. He was too complex. There would always be something to contend with. Some new facet to think about. The thought was exciting.

She stared back at his direct, challenging look. "You'd like to get rid of me, wouldn't you? Well, you can't. We're stuck with each other merely because we chose the same isolated stretch of geography to crash on. I'm not that bad, am I? I like you."

Joe hated that her words touched his heart. The very same one that he thought had turned to stone. The very same one that he had hoped would turn to dust. He reached across the table and picked up a lock of hair that fell over her shoulder. "I didn't say you were bad. You're crazy, you're a pain, but you're not bad." He wanted to know what happened back there to make her withdraw so quickly. He wanted to know why he even cared. He tried again. "Something happened back there in the restaurant. What was it?"

She finished her food and balled her trash. He took it from her and pitched it the same as he had his, only this time he missed. He walked over and picked it up. Then she was there, beside him, ready to move on. He let it pass that she ignored his question.

The sounds of the ocean, the sea gulls, and the taste of the good food, badly prepared, seemed to have a settling effect on Sterling. She sighed and looked around.

After gathering her bag they walked side by side down the old, warped and worn plankboard dock looking at the boats. The feel of his guiding hand on the small of her back was unnerving her. She was vulnerable right now. Out of nowhere, a feeling, a memory had came flying by and knocked her back in time. Five years.

She concentrated on strolling beside Joe, forced herself to let the sights and smells bring her back to the present. She would have liked to just lean on Joe, lean into him and have a good cry. She deserved it. She needed it. She reached a hand out and tucked it in his arm. When he hugged it to him, she was surprised. It was a gesture of possession. A gesture of caring. She leaned her cheek against his shoulder, grateful that he let her. Grateful that he asked no more questions.

Crab nets hung on the boats. The smell of bait and salt, fish, and old, wet wood permeated the air. Joe stood by silently as Sterling chatted with an old sailor and asked questions about his work. He marveled to himself how she could really be interested in all these little things. She had such a zest for life . . . was so full of living that it just seemed to burst from her. And there wasn't a man or woman that talked to her that didn't enjoy it. When the one old man gave her a torn section of his fishing net as a souvenir, she planted a kiss on his cheek. He blushed and turned back to his work hurriedly.

Joe indulged her when she insisted on sitting on the end of the dock, their feet dangling over the edge, Huck Finn style.

Joe teased. "That old man is going to go home and make love to his wife tonight."

"Joe." She elbowed him and blushed. "He's a sweet old man."

"He's a man. And you're a pretty young woman. That kiss took him back to his early years. You made his day. Maybe his year." He was holding back a chuckle as she pretended to shun him. His shoulder was touching hers. Her thigh was close. He could feel the female aura surround him. He wanted to put his arm around her shoulders, feel her rest her head against him, but something kept him from initiating the movement toward her. He picked up a pebble from the dock and pitched it into the water.

Taking the time to unwind and let her mind go blank was exactly what she needed. She kept her thinking to a minimum and simply enjoyed watching the gulls play and the sunlight sparkle across the water. She listened to the occasional chatter of the fishermen; heard them unloading wooden tubs, dragging nets from one place to another.

Each movement had a purpose, no steps were wasted as they snugged their boats for the night.

Later, they climbed the steps back toward the row of shops. Joe closed his fingers around hers and noticed the wistfulness in her eyes as she looked up at him and smiled.

He took her arm. "I'm tired. It's getting late." He didn't look at his watch. He didn't wear one. Time apparently had no meaning to him. "I didn't notice a theater in this town. We could watch one of your movies or stop and rent one."

Sterling was tiring, too, but it was more mental. Joe had made a nice gesture offering the food and sunshine. She almost didn't want to go back just now, but the idea of curling up on her comfortable overstuffed sofa sounded like heaven.

"Yes. Let's. We're sure to find a video store in Ocean City, and we do have to feed your babies."

He grunted at that information but found that he wasn't all that uncaring about the projected evening. He would have to be careful, though. He was beginning to feel too manly again. He was recognizing the fact that she was having an effect on him. Maybe it was good, maybe it wasn't. He still didn't know who had sent her or why. He still didn't know if she was for real or some cruel trick of fate. He still couldn't identify the feelings she stirred in him; wasn't sure he should.

As they approached the jewelry store owned by the sweet old folks, their attention was immediately drawn to two young men making a hasty but hopefully unobtrusive exit from the shop. Each man held a feed sack as they dashed from the shop toward their old, battered yellow pickup truck.

Sterling felt Joe tense beneath the hand she had tucked in the crook of his elbow. Their suspicions were confirmed at the exact time the elderly lady came shuffling out of the shop, her fist raised in the air.

Her voice was almost lost over the roar of the pickup

as it started moving away from the curb. "Help. Somebody stop them. They robbed us!" Her husband was right behind her, putting an arm around her trying to coax her back into the store. She'd have none of it. She stood on the sidewalk and continued to shake her fist at the two men jumping in the truck, tears rolling down her pink cheeks.

The entire scenario was in jerky slow motion, like a very old newsreel at a Saturday afternoon matinee. Sterling would have sworn to it. She was nailed to the spot by disbelief and shock as were the other people who slowly became aware of what was going on. She wanted to move . . . she wanted to stop them. She felt instinctively that Joe would click into action.

Sterling pulled her arm free from Joe, figuring he would make a run for them now. There were only two of them and he could surely catch them quickly enough. The truck wasn't making much headway as the driver revved the engine and pulled the stick into gear, grinding it.

She found her voice, "Joe! Get them! Don't let them get away!"

The wheels peeled rubber as the truck skidded away from the curb and down Main Street. People stood riveted to their spots, staring disbelievingly. Other shopkeepers came to the sidewalk to talk among themselves and offer kind words to the proprietors. Kids soon ignored the incident and went back to their games.

Suddenly Sterling could feel her pulse tripping at her temple. Her throat was dry and she felt the anger and indignation that came with the realization of what she was witnessing. She turned to look at Joe, to try to understand why he hadn't made an attempt to stop the thieves. She couldn't hide her disappointment. She didn't even try. Joe returned her stare. He seemed to have completely distanced himself from her . . . from what just happened.

Sterling slapped a killing look on Joe and went into the

shop to help settle the couple. The elderly man was calling the police.

The little old lady was crying, weeping into a lacy handkerchief and sitting on a stool in the back room. Sterling put her hands on the woman's shoulders and hugged her. "They'll find them. They'll get your money back." She tried to smile up at Sterling through teary eyes only to break down again. Her husband came back to hold her hand.

"They took our wedding rings," she cried anew. "It wasn't enough that they took all they could, they had to take our rings. We've had those rings for over fifty years." She wept uncontrollably into her husband's shirt.

He looked over her head and smiled at Sterling. "She'll be all right. You don't have to stay with us."

"Did they have guns?" Sterling asked, wondering how close they had all come to death.

"Said they did. We didn't take the chance. It's not worth our lives. Hush now, Sadie. It'll not change a thing."

Sterling felt so sorry for them. It was obvious they had worked hard together for a long, long time, and now two thugs had come in here and changed their lives. More, she was angry with Joe. They'd been violated, and right under a policeman's nose. He could have stopped all of this, but he hadn't.

She couldn't understand it. It didn't make any sense at all.

"Thank you for your concern, young lady. Your husband is waiting for you. It's okay. There's nothing you can do."

Her husband. A natural assumption, but her reaction was not natural. It sent a chill of the unknown up her spine. "I saw them. If you need any witnesses, just call this number." She handed him her card after she hastily penciled in the number at the cottage.

The sidewalk was devoid of Joe. She looked this way

and that. Guessing that he'd gone to the car, Sterling squared her shoulders. She gathered her stuff, smoothed her skirt, and headed to where they parked the car. She was furious. The thugs had managed to get lots of money and all the jewelry they could scoop up. The poor old folks were so upset and shocked . . . and scared it might happen again. Their lives would be in a mess for a while. And Joe. Mighty Joe the Cop did nothing. He hadn't even tried.

She was angry. She was appalled. She was disappointed. He was in her car behind the wheel. She stopped in front of the shiny vehicle and glared at him. "How could you? You could easily have nabbed one of them. At least they would have stood a chance of regaining some of their merchandise."

Lighting a cigarette, Joe barely glanced up. "You want to get in the car? You're causing a scene."

"I'll cause one if I want to. How dare you be so complacent when you had the ability to do something? Get out from behind the wheel." She banged the hood of the Porsche with her bag.

"I'm driving home. Now, get in," he ordered.

She stood a moment longer, trying to regain some semblance of composure. She wasn't sure she wasn't going to bop him a good one when she sat down beside him.

He sat silently, waiting. He wasn't going to listen to any of her bull. He wasn't a cop any longer and he wasn't going to take on the problems of the world for the rest of his life. Those creeps would be caught and most of the jewelry recovered. The courts would slap them on the wrist and set them free in a short time, anyway. Stuff like this was somebody else's trouble for a change. He was tired of it. And he didn't want another investigation. He didn't want to answer any more questions. Besides, the old people had to have insurance. It wasn't his problem.

She slammed herself into the passenger seat and jerked

the seat belt on. "If you're driving, do it and forget stopping for the movies. I'm not in the mood."

Nor was he. Joe shot the car out of the parking space and drove with great concentration. Once on the open highway he let the car cruise at seventy.

"You're speeding," she said nastily.

He wasn't sure he liked her temper. She could be just as mad as she was happy and he didn't want to have to handle that or anything right now. He didn't like himself. He didn't like her. The urge had been there. His policeman's heart and training had told him to collar those two-bit jerks. It was almost another way of punishing himself. To keep from doing it. That realization hit him. He hadn't thought of his self-imposed isolation as punishment. He hadn't thought about it at all until this deranged woman had come on the scene. He didn't have to take any of this.

"They were the nicest old people. Still so in love and contented and now . . . now they've been violated." She looked out the window and tried to calm down.

Sterling realized she was overreacting to this entire day. It wasn't just the robbery. It was also the little boy. She rubbed her hand over her eyes. She wanted to be alone. She wanted time to think all this out and get out from under this feeling of loss. Could it be that Joe was reawakening feelings of love that she had simply isolated and channeled toward helping other people and then merely continuing her own way?

Concentrating on the passing scenery, Sterling wondered why all these buried feelings were stirring now. She had managed to think of Jerry and Timmy other times without the pain being so searing. Had her compassion for Joe poked a stick into her own feelings and mixed them up?

She rolled the window down in defense against his furious puffing on his cigarette. It was dark now. Dark and cloudy. A light rain sprinkled the windshield. The road was dangerous. The headlights picked up the warning of slippery conditions.

"Took their wedding rings, too. Had them for fifty years or more." She pouted with vehemence as the injustice of it hit her again.

The silence in the car hung heavily. He flipped the radio on and she immediately switched it off.

Because there was no use trying to suppress it, she snapped, "You should have done something, Joe . . . you should have."

"Damn it, am I going to have to listen to this all the way back to the beach? I don't even know why I'm here with you. How did I end up being so stupid as to even suggest we go up there? I'm losing my mind. That's all there is to it. Now shut up and let me drive this dandy little car home in peace." He had no defense, so attack was called for. He hated this, he hated everything. "Do you hear yourself? Did you hear yourself back there on the sidewalk ordering me around like a German shepherd?" He wanted a stiff drink. Hell, he wanted four.

She had heard and wasn't exactly proud of it, but there was no stopping it. "Yes, you are going to have to listen to this all the way home." She felt him accelerate to eighty. "What you did was wrong and insensitive. Why didn't you help them?" she demanded, pounding a fist on her knee.

He remained silent and she watched the speedometer go up to eighty-five, then ninety. The blood pulsed in her head. First the little boy, then the old people . . . and it all went right by Joe. He didn't even care that those people lost their money. He didn't even care that the dumb little kid almost broke her heart. Then she quickly admonished herself from that thought. He had no way of knowing the effect the tot had on her insides. But it was the only thing that wasn't his fault.

Okay, she admitted to herself. *I'm not being reasonable.*

I'm not being rational. But something had snapped inside her and she had yet to get control.

She didn't like that he was speeding. It scared her more than a little since it was so dark and traffic had increased.

"Right, kill me, too, now." As soon as the words were out of her mouth she could have slid under the seat and hid.

Sterling could feel the power of his anger. The cockpit of the car filled with it. He slammed the brakes on, making her claw for the dashboard. With a squeal of tires and a direct swerve, the car fishtailed to a dangerous halt on the side of the road.

"I don't need this. Drive the damn car yourself and be quiet while you're doing it." He opened his car door and Sterling had a momentary pang of concern for him as the traffic whizzed by. And then he was on her side, opening her door and motioning for her to get out and get in on the other side.

Ignoring him, she hiked up her skirt so she could scoot over and under the steering wheel. Casting him a glacial look, she drove on the shoulder of the road until she built up some speed and then, turning the signal on, melted into the stream of cars.

The silence was deafening. She could hear his breathing. Hear him light another cigarette and slide the window down a little. She didn't dare look at him.

Reaching the cottage at last, Sterling didn't think she could keep quiet much longer. She parked the Porsche in front of her door. They both got out of the car and slammed the doors.

They stared at each other over the hood of the car through the darkness for long moments, the mist cloaking both of them.

She shifted and held her bag with both hands. She felt like crying and tilted her chin to ward it off. After all, he was the one retreating from life. Why did she have to accept that without a fuss?

She heard Joe's barely audible sigh and muttered curse and wondered what she should do now. Now that she had royally screwed up everything with her temper and her swirling feelings. He was standing there, looking at her through the darkness. Words were on the tip of her tongue. But they would probably be the wrong words again.

"You were wrong. You're still a cop. Nothing has changed that. Nothing but you." She felt the fresh sting of tears behind her eyes. "Red would hate this. I just bet he would."

Joe merely stood there in the shadows, the sounds of the ocean behind him.

She ought to help him feed the kittens. They would all be very hungry. But he could do it himself. She stomped over the sand, and went inside her own cheery cottage.

After she showered and dried her hair she parted the curtains just a little and saw that he still had lights on. She puttered around, straightening things that didn't need it and wondering. Wondering if she was doing more harm than good. Never did she doubt herself more than on this job.

She walked over to the phone. This could all be ended. It could be over. She could call Ramsburg and tell him she wasn't qualified to help this man. He needed professional help, or at least unbiased help. She realized then that she would have to tell him that Joe T. MacDaniels was becoming too important to her. That she was becoming too involved in making him happy; too caught up in making herself happy.

Her hand hovered over the receiver. Pulling away from it, she simply reminded herself that she'd called Joe a quitter. That would make her the same thing and nothing . . . nothing would be solved at all.

She flipped the lights off as she walked around the room. It was midnight. A fog had settled in over the ocean, clouding the windows with mist. She slid the door open to the deck and let the cool air wash over her. She

didn't want to leave. A man she knew only a few days
. . . she didn't want to leave him.

Sterling looked up toward the sky. All haze. Nothing
clear. No definite line between earth and atmosphere. She
knew what was out there, she just couldn't find it right
now. Tomorrow it would be there. Tomorrow.

Joe pushed the box of kittens back near the sink. Damn
her. Damn her. She was getting to him. It might be in
bits and pieces, but she was peeling away layers of him
and reaching in, touching him, drawing him back into the
human race. He didn't want that. He didn't want to feel
the things that crawled around inside him. It was easy
before she came. Easy to cancel life. Easy to forget all
the things he wanted out of life. There was something
about her . . . He fixed himself a drink and turned out the
lights as he walked through the house. Sliding the door
back, he walked to the deck.

He was angry at himself for hurting her. She mattered
to him. The exact moment at which she began to be important to him was evasive, but she definitely made him feel
things . . . things that would have been better left alone.
Sterling Powell. He pictured her the way she looked
whirling out of the shop with those silly clothes on, the
way she talked to the sailor and made him smile. He
remembered the way she felt when she tucked her arm
through his and leaned against him . . . the way her hair
smelled.

It seemed he was always angry at himself lately. Red.
What would he think about all this? Suppose it had been
Red who had shot *him*. He would have the support of
family and friends. He would have survived. Joe remembered the night before the accident.

They had closed a job. Finished it with success and
they were at Roper's, the local pub, celebrating. Red sat
across from him popping peanuts in his mouth and making
remarks about the female bartenders that he didn't mean.

He loved his wife, was completely satisfied with his life, but that didn't stop him from admiring beautiful women.

Red had always liked to toy with the English language. He raised his beer bottle to Joe and toasted. "Here's to the baddest cops in town. We done good."

"That we did," Joe agreed, and they had clinked bottles dangerously hard and chugged them dry. And they had laughed and slapped each other on the back and tipped their chairs back on the rear legs. They had control of the world. They felt invincible. They were unconquerable.

And then twenty-four hours later, Red lay in his arms, bleeding all over him.

He lifted the glass to his lips and drained it. Bringing his arm back and then swinging forward, he tossed the empty glass over the sand and into the water.

SIX

Pulling her lawn chair to the edge of the deck, Sterling sat down and propped her feet on the bottom rail. Opening her book, she laid it in her lap, but instead of looking at it, she watched the gulls and let them take her with them on their flight for sustenance and sunrise exercise.

Last night's clouds lingered here and there, drawing dark, hazy lines across the reddening horizon where the sun floated up. It appeared to be smiling.

The strong rays chased the chill from her bare arms and legs. She felt the urge to strip and run naked over the sand. Freedom. Liberty. Abandonment. She smiled. She was bold but not that intrepid. She wished she could be.

Yesterday she had avoided Joe completely, which was easy since she hadn't seen any sign of him. He needed time to think. Needed time to evaluate. If she had made a dent in his protective armor, then so much the better.

She made it a point not to look toward Joe's cottage. Still, she couldn't keep her thoughts at bay. She had lost her temper with him and she didn't like that. A good forthright mad was okay, but she didn't like it when her nature kept working her mouth.

How did a man learn to live with danger every day? What did it do to him? What did it do to those who loved him?

She automatically turned her head toward his cottage the minute she heard his door slide open. He came out dressed only in jeans. She watched as he walked to the steps and looked out to sea, his hands in his pockets. His hair blew when the breeze crossed his face. He was handsome. Almost magnificent. Her heart fluttered, and she wondered if feeling like a teenager in love for the first time was possible. The anticipation was there again. Sterling picked up her Stephen King and tried to read the words. The next move was up to Joe.

In her peripheral vision, she saw him go back inside. *Oh, well*, she sighed to herself. *Maybe it wasn't.*

Returning to the kitchen, she pulled a box of cereal from the cupboard and grabbed a quart of milk from the refrigerator.

Sterling stopped short from sprinting up onto the deck. Joe was just inside the door with a gun in his hand. After her first rush of breath she could see that he was cleaning it. Feeling foolish, she drew her lips into a smile and bounced through the open door. "Morning."

He grunted. "Stop by some other time. Like when you're on your way out of Ocean City to say good-bye."

"It's going to be a wonderful day. What do you want to do?"

He pushed the gun-cleaning equipment under the couch and went into his bedroom to replace his gun. When he returned, he watched her setting the table in his kitchen with her breakfast materials.

"Just what I'm doing. Nothing."

"Nope. You did that yesterday." She sat down and gestured for him to join her. He sidled over to the sink and leaned on the counter. "So you're over your little snit and you think you can come in here like nothing happened."

She poured milk over her cereal and used her spoon to bury the Cheerios in it. "Basically. Come on. I went to a lot of trouble to prepare the breakfast of champions. The least you can do is eat it."

"Wheaties are the breakfast of champions."

"Come eat, Joe." She leveled a spoonful of sugar over her bowl.

He turned his back on her and set up the baby bottles. He proceeded to fill them and pull the box of kittens over to the couch. Plopping down, Joe reached in and picked one of them up. He pretended to be very interested in what he was doing. She was being dismissed again.

"You can ignore me all you want. I'm not going away."

"I don't care what you do," he grumbled.

Sterling got up and snatched one of the bottles from the sink. Picking up one of the kittens, she went out onto the deck and sat on the top step. When she had finished feeding it, she placed the kitten on the deck and watched it crawl around. She ran a finger down the soft fur and encouraged it to explore.

Joe came out on the deck and scooped the kitten up and returned it to its box. "You tried to feed me and you fed the cat, now go home, Sterling. I don't need Mother Superior around all day."

"That's not very neighborly of you, Joe."

"I'm not neighborly. And I'm not your knight in shining armor. You know that by now. Just leave me alone. If I'm screwing up your job, that's your problem. If you're here on vacation, then just do what you were planning on doing—without me. I'm not dependable, remember?"

"I wasn't going to bring up the incident. Why are you?"

"Because it's a something-nothing."

She looked up at him then. "You mean it's something that means nothing or nothing that means something?"

He snorted. "Would the robbery have occurred whether we were there or not?"

"Yes. It would have happened regardless."

He shrugged. "Something-nothing."

She smiled at him and he continued to watch the waves. "Maybe you're right. But that's over. I've already been busy this morning. There's a dinner cruise tonight. I'm not going to go alone. I made reservations for both of us."

He turned to look at her. She had let her head fall back a little, to catch the direct rays of the sun. Her hair streamed down behind her, curling and soft. Inviting. Her eyes were closed, but he knew the animation that would fill them.

"I don't think so."

She opened her eyes to slits. "I can't very well go without an escort. Well, I *could*, but I prefer not to. I know. You can't dance. That's why you don't want to go."

"You're probably right."

When he just lit a cigarette she sat up straight and looked at him. "The other day you decided where we would go. Today it's my turn. It's that simple. I'll teach you," she teased, knowing a man like him knew how to dance.

He blew a smoke ring. "Right." He watched it widen and disappear on a drift of wind.

Satisfied, Sterling smiled. He still wasn't looking at her. He watched the ocean curl and roll. He watched the gulls swoop for breakfast. Though he had merely finger-combed his hair and his eyes still held that haunted look that touched her so deeply, he was coming out of it. Slowly, but surely. If he didn't recognize it, she did.

She was pleased. When he had returned the gun to his room, he had pulled on a red tank top that complemented his muscled arms and shoulders. She knew the strength that was there extended to his spirit. She could even see the stirrings of it.

When he looked back at her, she smiled. He felt that tug in his stomach again. Sometime during the long sleepless night, during the hours of restlessness, he had felt it then, too. What was it about her that got to him when nothing else could? Because she was something good in his life. Something real and something nice. And because he saw a side of her the other day that told him she was hiding some wounds of her own.

The sun danced through her hair. A zest for life sparkled in her eyes. She might be a little bizarre, but if that's what it took to make Sterling Powell who she was, then who was he to question? Besides that, she took his vote over nightmares, a drunken stupor, and a bad book any day. Furthermore, maybe she needed him. Maybe she was recovering from some crisis of her own and needed him.

Sterling took her time to dress. She wanted to knock his eyes out tonight and she didn't stop to question exactly why. He was rejoining the living. If they could make it through this evening as any average couple . . . Couple? She smiled at herself in the mirror.

He came by way of the front door and pushed it open. "You ready?" He stopped when she came from the bedroom. She was beautiful. Her hair was piled on top of her head leaving long curls at her neck and ears. Her dress was a stunning emerald-green silk that caressed her body as it fell over the curves. The neckline dipped to a V and a long gold chain with a small emerald winked there. She had accented her eyes with something dark and tinted her mouth with just the slightest tint of pink. The image of the interfering imp disappeared and the reality of a lovely woman took place.

"You look very nice," she told him as she walked over to him. And he did. He was wearing a western-cut black sport coat, black slacks, and a black shirt with pearl snaps. A thin gray tie clipped with silver lay slightly crooked down the front. Straightening it for him, she caught the scent of his spicy aftershave. He was handsome and he looked indomitable.

"I never was any good with these things," he told her as her closeness contracted his muscles. "You're beautiful."

She stood back. "Thank you." She had to. The attraction she felt for him had leaped to a dangerous level. She had seen him at his worst and pretty close to his best. That alone made her feel an admiration for him. She just plain liked the man. He had a good heart and she felt things she couldn't describe radiate from him to her. It pulled at her. It didn't leave her alone.

She handed him the keys to the Porsche. He took them, offered her his arm, and together they went outside.

Sterling felt a pulse of excitement as they arrived at the dock. It was sundown and the ship was draped with colored lights. People strolled on board, chattering and laughing. Music floated on the air invitingly.

She felt his fingers curl around hers as they went up the gangplank. They were led to a table and seated. Their wineglasses were filled and then a deep voice welcomed them aboard over a grainy intercom system. The ship's horn blasted its signal and they were on their way.

They were one of at least twenty couples. Some were old, some young, some appeared to be on their honeymoon. Joe and Sterling took their drinks to the rail and watched as the mooring ropes were released and the boat glided out of port.

"I love this. Look, over there. I'd hate to wash all those windows."

He followed her gaze to the multistoried house that stood near the water's edge. Then turning back, he looked at her and watched the way she took in everything and found pleasure in it all: the jet skiers jumping the wake of their ship, the other small crafts that passed them, the passengers waving in response to her waves.

Dinner was lobster. He winced as she asked for more butter. The food was rich, the music soothing, and the company was lively. She chatted with other travelers.

Darkness fell, and with it came a bright, mysterious aura created by the lights and the music and the gentle sway of the boat. She declined dessert but stood up and offered Joe her hand. He took it and led her to the dance floor.

The moment he turned her into his arms, she knew he knew more about dancing than she could ever forget. One hand flattened and pressed against the middle of her back, the other took hers out and down. Holding her close, but inches away, he moved in a fluid and almost seductive way. Catching the beat, he stepped to the side, quarter step and pause . . . sway to the other side, quarter step and pause . . . forward and then back and hold. He turned his full attention to her and she looked into clear eyes, eyes that had forgotten their brooding look for just a little while and now searched her own, challenging and daring. Pure male sexuality exuded from him. Responding, she swayed and dipped. When he turned, she flowed.

Joe circled, pulling her body solidly against his own. The power filled her, enveloping both, combining them in a small world of their own filled with music and magic.

When he paused for several beats, keeping her mesmerized with his eyes, her stomach lifted, fluttered and floated. The pulse at her wrist tripped double-time. Excitement ran through her veins to bring a flush to her cheeks.

There was no smile on his lips. No gentleness in his eyes. Tightening his fingers around her own, he slowed his steps to no movement at all. Couples swirled all around them. They stood in the dance position, feeling. Just feeling.

Electricity traveled from her toes to her ears. He moved

to lay his jaw against her temple. Sterling's breath snagged.

She was all smooth motion under her hands. The silk whispered over her body as she moved. After pressing the lightest kiss on her cheek, he whispered, "When do the lessons begin?"

The light danced in her eyes as she smiled up at him. "Depends on who's teaching who, and what."

He wanted to lean forward and kiss her, but stepped back and twirled her out and back to him. She laughed and exaggerated the move.

Power. It possessed him. It motivated him in everything he did. An energy, a pulse that drove him . . . she could feel it. It excited her. The fact that a man of this caliber spent time with her, valued her even though he didn't trust her, calmed her.

The music changed, abruptly, deliberately, to a Virginia reel. Hoots and hollers rang out over the air as everyone took partners and began some real foot-stomping.

Sterling was stolen from Joe by an aging gentleman with blue-white hair and twinkling green eyes. She was whirled and twirled and bumped and pulled. She would join hands with Joe only to have him traded off to another partner. She didn't miss the smug look in his eyes.

After ten minutes of hoedown, the music returned to the soft, romantic, dreamy tunes. She and Joe found themselves back at their table. She was breathless and glowing.

"See. See. You *are* having a good time," she challenged him.

The darkness that floated into his eyes set her back. Just like that. One moment he was obviously enjoying it. The next . . . it was back again. What had she done?

It hit him. It hit him hard. The guilt. It was recognizable this time. All too evident. He was alive and his friend was dead. And he missed him. And he hated himself for what he did. A blackness took over and shrouded him from all the things going on around him. He signaled the waiter and ordered a double. Sterling watched him, alerted to something dangerous.

It was over. The fun, the excitement. Maybe it was too much, too soon. She had messed up again. "Joe?"

He shook his head and downed his drink. "How long before we dock?"

She checked her little velvet-strapped watch. "About half an hour. Are you okay?"

He seemed to take control of himself and forcibly push his way through the bleakness. "You wanted to dance. Let's do it."

But it was different now. He didn't look at her. His eyes roamed to the other couples, the tables, the abyss that surrounded the ship. She looked up at him, squeezed his hand, and waited for a response. There was none.

Sterling moved closer to him, knowing he wouldn't push her away in front of everyone out of simple manners. "Joe. Talk to me. Don't shut me out."

"Dance, Sterling. Just dance."

"You're letting it happen again. Fight it. It's the only way to get past it."

He stopped dead-still, his arm around her, her face inches from his. He seemed to be at war with something. She sensed there was something threatening to burst forth from him. He was like a caged animal.

He dropped her hand and stalked to the door leading to the bottom level. Sterling gave him a few moments and then she traced his steps. She found him leaning on the railing smoking a cigarette near the back of the ship. It was darker here. The hum of the motor and the sound of the sea rolling beneath secluded them even more. She walked up and leaned against his back.

When he turned, she was sure it was violence she saw in his eyes. He pulled her roughly to him and ground his mouth against hers. *Not this time*, she thought. She pulled back and stepped away from him, feeling just a little more than shaky.

Her eyes mirrored her thoughts. He wasn't going to treat her with complete disregard. Every time it got to him when she was around, he vented himself with her.

He held up his hand when she started to speak. "This isn't your fault. None of it is. Just leave me alone. Go back upstairs and wait for me. I'll be up in a minute." He turned his back to her and pitched his cigarette overboard.

She took a place by the railing next to him. The sounds of the music and the laughter reached her ears and made her envy the light-hearted enjoyment from inside.

"You need a friend, Joe. Why don't you let me be that person?"

"A friend? A friend wouldn't be here to get information any way she could get it. A friend would recognize when a man wants to be left alone and would leave him alone. A friend is what I had before I killed him."

She remained silent but didn't move away.

"He no longer knows the pleasure of his wife, the love of his kids, or the simple joy a man can get from being somewhere with someone he enjoys being with. The feeling of a woman in his arms and all night ahead of him." His words were directed at her, but he didn't look her way.

She let her breath out slowly. She felt the resentment even though she realized that his grief was too fresh. She remembered all too well how she felt for a long time after Jerry's death. She knew any sympathy she might offer him would only serve to feed his dark mood.

"A pity party. That's what this has turned into. I'm growing very weary of your self-pity. Self-flagellation is ugly. You're a man who has handled nasty things before and managed to get through them. Maybe even thrive on them. You haven't given in to the fact that your friend is dead. Have you cried?" At his dark glare she answered, "I thought not. Men do cry, Joe. They need to. It's a biological release. Maybe it's necessary before you can begin to heal."

He was silent a moment, and Sterling could almost feel him fighting back cruel words. She could feel him tense and draw on all the control he had available. She waited.

When he turned to her, he reached one hand up to touch a curl that fell to her shoulder. "I don't need you around to constantly be the voice of my own mind. Maybe I don't want you to point out what goes on inside me." His voice was strained and controlled. She was afraid he would lash out at her any moment. His touch caused her to be unsteady.

The ship's horn blasted. Bells chimed. A runabout swished past them. A wave caught the side of the boat and sprayed them in mist.

"Trust me, Joe. Hold on to me. I'm here. I've offered my friendship to you with no expectations, no boundaries. All you have to do is reach out and hold tight to the hand I have offered you."

He gathered her in his arms and crushed her to him. She felt the tremor roll through his body, knew from the way his breath caught that he was close to the release he needed. But it couldn't come here. She held him until they both steadied. "I'll go on up." She lifted to her tiptoes and placed a kiss on his chin.

Without another word, she left him there when all she wanted was to stay with him.

He opened the car door for her and rounded the hood. He'd been silent as he drove home. At the cottages, he parked the Porsche in front of her house and opened the door for her.

The moon was nearly full. It cast a daylight haze across the ocean and sand.

He escorted her to her door. "How much more material do you need for your story?"

She blew out her breath. "I start getting through to you and then you're gone. I thought you believed me. I thought for a moment on the ship that I had gained your trust.''

He took her by the shoulders and turned her until the moonlight fell full on her face. "The question is, what do you want from me? You keep putting yourself in my way. You keep looking at me with those eyes, you keep smiling at me with those lips . . . and you keep reaching out to me, and when I respond, it scares me. Because I don't understand it.''

He bent his head toward her slowly. His hand came up to frame her face. "I just want to touch you. Not even kiss you. I just want to touch you.''

His hand ran slowly down her neck, across her shoulder. He pulled the pins from her hair and tangled his fingers in it as it tumbled to her shoulders.

She trembled from his touch. The gentleness, the kindness that she sensed was there was so evident now. She caught her breath as he toyed with the gold hoops at her ears, the necklace that lay between her breasts.

She kept pushing the good part of life in his face, kept offering him something he felt incapable of accepting. He felt himself pulse with it. He watched her eyes as she looked at him, trusting him, and wondered how they would look when he let her down.

"I . . . I was pretty hard on you back there on the ship. It's just that I can't stand to see you torturing yourself.'' Because she knew she had to be, she was patient.

"Don't preach to me, Sterling. I've heard it all. Used some of it myself. I don't give a damn anymore. The hell with it. The hell with the whole world. Go back to where you came from. I don't want to deal with you anymore. You're a dreamer or a cunning conartist. Either way, I don't want any of it.''

"That's not true. I see it in your eyes.''

Her sweet voice, the acceptance in her smile, was too much. "I don't need this. I don't damn well need this.''

He turned from her and walked purposefully to his own cottage.

She stayed where she was for long moments after he had disappeared into his cottage. He snapped lights on as he went and she pictured him pouring himself a drink and then going about the routine of feeding the kittens.

She was in trouble. A new house or a new job wasn't going to fix this man's life. Walking over to his steps, she climbed them slowly. He had shed his jacket and kicked his boots in a corner. He was leaning over with both hands on the sink. She wanted to go to him—and what? Maybe things were better left alone for tonight. She turned to go and caught movement out of the corner of her eye between their two cottages. Looking again, she thought she saw someone duck back into the shadows.

Going down the steps, Sterling used the moonlight to guide her way up the sandy incline. Topping the hill, she saw a car pull away from the driveway with its lights off. Somewhere down the road, the headlights were punched on and the car drove away. Who would be snooping around? Kids, she decided. They were the only two cottages on this isolated strip of beach and probably some kids came down, cruising and into mischief. But she tried to shake off the uneasy feeling, remembering the car that had seemed to tail them the other day. It could all be a coincidence. She shrugged. It had to be.

SEVEN

Sterling woke to bright sunshine. Sitting up, she swung her feet to the floor. A new day. Maybe she could forget about the fitful night. She stood and stretched her tired muscles. Moving to the mirror over her dresser, she studied her reflection. Her eyes attested to her fatigue. Grimacing, she forced her mouth into a smile and talked to the image in the glass. "Up! Bright! Happy!" She frowned. "Forget it."

She dressed in pink shorts and a Mickey Mouse T-shirt, then braided her long hair. She'd decided to start the day with a run on the beach. It usually gave her a better perspective and made her feel invincible. She needed that feeling. As much for herself as for Joe Timothy MacDaniels. She pulled on her yellow high-top tennis shoes and jogged down the steps, a new, stronger resolution in her mind. She had a job to do. She was usually so good at her work. She had to get her mind back on business and keep it there.

The first thing she noticed was that his Jeep was gone.

She blinked and looked again. Gone! Now she'd done it. She ran to the bottom of his steps, taking them two at a time. She had been too harsh with him. She had acted like a crazy woman in Delaware, and then last night she had shown him too much about how she was feeling about him. He was right. He didn't need this. So he had left. Could she blame him? No. She had to blame herself.

She slid the door open and sprinted into the living room. It was then she heard them. The soft, begging mewing that said, "Feed me." He had left the kittens? He was without a heart. Then she saw the normal things lying around. His clothes were still draped over everything that would support something; the sink was still full of dirty dishes, the remains of the vodka bottle lay in a pile where he had swept it; the broom was propped against the wall.

Walking over to the box that served as home and mother to the orphaned felines, she stepped on a wet towel. Picking it up, she realized it was soaked with baby formula. Checking the trash can, she found the empty container. He had spilled it. She smiled when she pictured him, getting up, running his hands through his hair as he did so often, preparing little bottles . . . the ones lined up one, two, three on the sink and then dropping the can.

She could almost hear him swear, see him throw the towel over the mess, and then turn to search for his Jeep keys in the disarray around him. The relief that flooded through her surprised her. The job would have been over had he left, at least until she contacted Ramsburg to see if he wanted her to chase him around the country. She knew at that moment just how important Joe had become to her. She would have gone after him on her own. It was more now. And that was something else she would have to contend with.

But not now. She would take advantage of his absence and tidy things up a bit. She filled the sink and squirted soap into it. As the bubbles built, she dropped in dishes, glasses, and empty ashtrays. Going over to the kitten's box, she stroked them with a finger. "Soon Daddy will be home with your milk. Daddy." She laughed. *I'm sure he would appreciate that title*, she thought wryly.

She sorted clothes, dirty from clean, and dropped a load in the ancient washer. Taking his clean ones, she headed for his closet to deposit them on the shelf. A box was there. Just a simple cardboard box. His personal belongings, she guessed. Her hand moved to open it, but something stopped her.

She pushed the vacuum around, wiped the end tables clear of ashes and water rings, arranged his paperback books on a shelf and stacked the magazines beside them. Washing the few dishes took only minutes. After transferring the clothes from washer to dryer she turned to the curtain rod that hung by one nail. Searching the drawers in the kitchen area, she found a hammer and rehung the curtains.

Sterling ran next door to her place to bring back her portable radio and turned on a country western station. She smiled. Everything looked so homey. Maybe the little bit of order she had restored would ease him some.

She gave the bathroom a quick once-over, then ended up standing in the doorway to his bedroom. The table beside the window held an empty glass, several books, and two overflowing ashtrays. One pillow was on the floor. The sheet and light blanket were twisted tornado-like down the middle of the bed. The bottom sheet was popped off one corner. It was then she noticed the small handgun on the night stand. It was positioned for instant reach. She walked over to it, ran her fingers down it.

It was cold. It was hard. She picked it up gingerly. Held it in the palm of her hand. It didn't scare her as she thought it might. She wrapped her fingers around it making sure not to put any pressure on the trigger. Instinct told her it was loaded. She looked at it, then she looked at herself holding it. Sterling tried to imagine herself using it on a human being. She couldn't. It had to take a special kind of person to do some things in life that were absolutely necessary. Or the right circumstances.

She was glad there were men like Joe and Red. Men who shouldered the responsibility, be it war, the protection and preservation of the rights of a free country, or the fight to protect innocent people from the madness and nastiness that existed in the world.

She replaced the gun exactly and shrugged. He had his reasons for making it readily available. Habit. A gun had been an extension of his hand for a long time. Why should he sever it now?

Sterling thought about making up the bed, but decided against it. There was something too intimate about that. The box in the closet struck her mind again. She would be violating his privacy . . . but then again, perhaps there was something in there that would answer some of the questions she had about him. No, she turned back into the living room. She couldn't do it.

She hadn't heard him drive up over the high volume of the music. She hadn't heard him walk up the steps, across the deck, and into the living room. But there he was with a bright green-and-pink boogie board tucked under one arm.

He looked at her and then around him. "What do you think you're doing?" That look again. She had seen it twice before. One that could accuse and shame, question, and cause doubt. Intimidate.

With her hands clasped behind her back, she smiled. "You can imagine my surprise when I saw your Jeep was gone . . . I thought you had just packed up and left. I couldn't blame you, the way I ran on last night. But I came up here and you weren't gone . . . just off to replace the formula you dropped. I was glad," she rattled on. "So, while I was waiting I figured I'd clean up a bit. I didn't think you'd mind. You've not been in the mood to do housework and . . . What's that?"

He had stood still, not smiling. He'd seen her come

from his bedroom and wondered if she'd had fun snooping. "I don't like my dirt moved. I go to great pains to get it where it is. When the clutter ticks me off, I'll clean it. Leave it alone."

Color drained from her face. He was serious. He must even wake up nasty. Then she realized what was really bothering him. "If you're wondering if I got into your personal stuff, the answer is no. But I did handle the gun on your nightstand. Just out of curiosity, and I was careful not to touch the trigger. It's a nice little gun. I dusted it."

"Don't ever get into that box in my closet. You had no business doing any of this. And that 'little gun' is a Jennings .22 automatic and it's loaded with stingers. Hinkley shot Reagan and Brady with one exactly like it. Don't handle that nice little gun."

He was dressed all in black. Standing in the doorway with the sun to his back, the daylight shot out from all sides. She was reminded of a gunslinger. Except for the boogie board he still held under his arm. In his other hand was a bag of groceries.

She shrugged. "Sorry." She pulled one of her braids around to tug on it. "Why did you get a boogie board?"

It was then he remembered it. He propped it on the couch and proceeded to the kitchen. Putting the bag on the clean countertop he said, over his shoulder, "It's for you."

"For me?" She jumped toward it and picked it up. "How do you do it? Oh, that was so nice of you to buy me one. Want me to help you feed the babies before we go?"

He held the can of formula half out of the bag and turned to look at her. "Before we go where?"

"Why, surfing, of course. You have to teach me." She joined him by the sink and held up one of the bottles for him to fill. He looked at her for a moment and then, taking the can opener, split the top of the formula package. She filled the bottles as he unloaded the grocery bag.

Sliding the kitty box to the couch, she took one bottle and one kitten and handed it to Joe, who came to sit beside her. "You should name them, you know. Everything has to have an identity. How about Shadow. He's so pretty and gray."

"He's a she and her name is Antoinette. After Marie."

Sterling laughed, and held up the orange kitten poking the little nipple into its mouth. "Who's this?"

"Elliott, T.S., and the other one is Chopin, Frederick."

"Elliott, Chopin, and Antoinette. Nothing like giving them something to live up to. I think we should leave them in the living room for a while today, instead of in the darkness of your kitchen. What do you think?"

"I think you talk too much. But yes, they can have sunshine for today." They settled back and continued the feeding. The silence was an easy one.

The kittens put down for a nap, she clapped her hands together and picked up the board. "Okay, first lesson."

"Go home, Sterling."

"But I thought . . ." She took one step back.

"Go home and change into your swimsuit first. I brought sandwiches from the restaurant and a bottle of wine. I found a nice cove a little way down. I figured we could have a picnic and you could ride the waves to your heart's content."

This abrupt change was par for the course and she should have been used to it, but it still took her by surprise. Her face broke into a grin. "I have a blanket we can take and a basket for the food if you need it."

He nodded, a smile playing at the corners of his handsome mouth. "Sometime during the night I decided I might be wrong about you. In any case, I think we'll take today to get to know each other better. Then I'll decide."

"Will you now?" She squared her shoulders. "Prepare yourself for a day you'll not soon forget, Joe MacDaniels. Because I've decided you are not going to leave the human race without a fight from me. The fact that I see a smile now and again is all the encouragement I need.''

She hoped he didn't see the wave of guilt that washed over her. She hoped he didn't see the surge of love that kept swooping in from nowhere. She hadn't figured any of this out yet, and she didn't want him to have even a hint that she was anything other than his self-imposed friend and neighbor.

"If I decided what I wanted was to leave the human race, there would be nothing you could do about it, Sterling."

She slammed a smile on him and was out the door in a flash leaving him standing there listening to the echo of his own words.

When she returned she was dressed in the two-piece bathing suit she had forced herself into bringing at Ramsburg's needling. It was black with a slash of orange neon. She felt self-conscious until his blatant appraisal of her told her she must still look all right in it.

Joe felt a tightening of all his muscles. She was a beautiful little imp. Bossy, overbearing, scatterbrained, and lovely. Always bright and never still, colorful and warm. He was reminded of candles on a cake.

Sterling watched Joe as he packed the basket she had brought back with her. He was wearing cut-off jeans for a bathing suit. His legs appeared strong, roped with muscles, hairy . . . and white. His upper torso was tanned, but she could tell he didn't get out of his jeans and into a bathing suit very often. "You sure look pretty," she said.

He turned to glare at her. "Men are not pretty. They're handsome."

"Well, you look handsome then." At his slow, devilish smile, she grinned back and changed the subject. "Did you pack any paper plates and napkins?"

"Always the den mother? Yes. They're packed." He picked up the basket while she took the blanket and the board. "After you." He followed her, which provided him a satisfactory view of the way her swimsuit clung to the curve of her bottom and a good look at her long smooth legs and her bare back. She had tied her hair up on top of her head and some strands lay loosely at her neck. He wondered what it would be like to kiss the soft flesh there.

He moved to walk beside her after they left the steps, shaking his head. This was even more unnerving. She had the blanket under one arm and the board under the other. The top of the suit barely hid the gentle swell of her breasts as she turned her face to smile up at him.

Joe MacDaniels, you must be crazy, a little voice said to him in his mind. But he didn't listen. Not today. The voice, the one that taunted him in his dreams, reminded him that he shouldn't be alive, was pushed far back into the recesses of his brain. Today was for nothing. Nothing at all. He'd contend with everything else later. For now, he was just going to try to relax and enjoy her company. And of course, find out once and for all who she was and what she wanted.

The cove was a half-mile walk from her place. She'd passed it on her first day there. Huge rocks, grass and sand over the top and around made a cozy little alcove just perfect for picnics. They spread the blanket, weighting the corners to keep the light breeze from flapping it around. The sun was hot, holding the promise of becoming even hotter. September weather was very unpredictable, but today was going to be a fine one.

"Okay. How do you ride one of these things?"

"You have to get in the water first," he directed as he walked into the ocean. The water was icy. Frigid. He heard her squeals beside him as she found out the same thing for herself.

They were up to their waists; the water swirled about them making them sway. Sterling braced her feet apart and tried to keep her balance. "This is powerful stuff. It wants to knock me over."

"Don't get too far away from me. You have to respect the strength of the sea and not test it. Next wave that comes, dive into it and get yourself adjusted to the temperature. Now!" he shouted, and she followed his lead and dived into the oncoming wave. She came up on the other side of it, spitting saltwater and shivering.

"This is nasty," she sputtered.

"You're not supposed to drink it. Now take the board with you and pick the next wave coming in. Turn, jump on the board, belly down, and ride the crest all the way to the shore."

She looked at him. "Right. I'll watch you a couple of times first."

Ride a boogie board? He thought not. Then he thought again. Why the hell not? He shrugged and, lying on the board, paddled out a little farther. She had trouble keeping her balance, but she watched his every move and then shouted with glee as he swept past her, riding the wave all the way to the sand.

He handed her the board when he came back out, but she shook her head. "Not yet. Do more. I'm studying." *And admiring.*

Joe had forgotten how abandoned it felt. Out here, surrounded by nothing but wind and surf, a man could forget who he was. He had forgotten the exhilaration of freedom that came from doing everyday things. He paddled a little farther out and then swept past Sterling again, this time standing on the board. She yelled and clapped as he went swooshing by. Now it was her turn.

The first time she tried it she lost the wave and the board. He didn't come to help her, simply stood by and watched her, nodding his encouragement. Three more times she lost the board and then, whoosh, she stayed on it, no matter how precarious, and rode the thing all the way onto the beach. Holding the board over her head, she shouted in triumph and headed out to join him again.

Joe smiled. It was the first smile that came from deep inside in a long time. It wasn't entirely unpleasant. The sun felt good on his face. The sea felt good swirling across his legs. His heart felt good watching the woman with the boogie board try to stand on it and almost knock herself out with it.

Sterling fast became exhausted. The ocean worked her like exercise class. The board cooperated only when it wanted to, and she grew tired. Her eyes stinging from the salt and her heart pounding from the exertion, she swam the board over to him. "Hang on, it'll take us in in no time."

He put his arms across it opposite hers. Flesh touched flesh, slippery with water. Faces close, they floated into shore. She was happy. Happier than she had been in a long, long time. "Thanks, Joe."

He ran a fingertip across her lips. She wanted to lean closer and kiss his mouth. She wanted to feel the soft brush of his mustache against her face. She wanted to lean into him and feel the power that was there. She wanted to be cocooned in his arms until the world went away. Just for a little while.

They propped the board against the rock and collapsed onto the blanket, laughing and tired.

Lying on the blanket next to him, she still felt the motion of the sea. It was a long time before she settled, then she wasn't sure some of her restlessness wasn't caused by the man lying silently next to her. She had begun to think he had fallen asleep when his hand found hers. Covered it.

Soaring. Floating. It was such a simple gesture. Really, not a big thing, but the feel of his hand holding hers . . . She smiled and turned her hand over so she could clasp his. She didn't speak for fear it would break whatever mellow mood he had fallen into. They lay there, side by side for long minutes. His thumb rubbed the back of her hand. She squeezed his fingers.

"I suppose you're hungry now," he said lazily. They both had their eyes closed against the blaring sunlight.

"Not just yet." She didn't want to break the contact. It was warming her, calming yet exciting, knowing yet unknowing.

This was hard to believe. She wasn't hungry yet? He smiled inwardly. She didn't want to move any more than he did. As long as they were where they were, as they were, no talking was needed, no questions would be asked and no answers given. If only this could last. But it couldn't. They were real people in an all too real world. But for now it was enough.

"You're going to get terribly sunburned," he murmured, letting his gaze wander over her exposed flesh.

"Umm," she answered, not caring.

"I brought some sun block," he offered, resisting the urge to touch her.

"That was thoughtful of you." *And sweet*, she thought.

"Won't help if you don't put it on," he persisted. He liked to watch the way her lips curved in a smile.

"Shut up, MacDaniels. You're breaking the spell." She sighed loudly and put her other hand under her head to get a little more comfortable.

"Spell? You are a witch! That would answer a lot of questions I have about you." She could hear the restrained smile in his voice.

"Oh, yeah. What questions do you have?"

"Why aren't you married? You're not completely horrid to look at. And I judge you to be around thirty. Most women are married with kids, up to their hips in laundry, involved in the PTA." He couldn't conjure up a picture of her doing those things.

His words hurt, but not like they would have in a different situation. Here with the sounds of eternity all around her, it didn't crush her so. "Not everyone is," she said, choosing not to get into it just now.

"Evasive answer, Powell. I'll try another one. Do you like being a secretary? It seems a bit tame for you."

"It's a job, and a well-paying one I might add. I know my stuff. I get to travel and see things and learn things I might never get a chance to do anywhere else." She ventured a question of her own. "Tell me what it's like to be a cop. I'm sure it's rewarding, but it's got to be a lot of hard work and I know the pay is nothing compared to the danger."

She felt his fingers tense and then relax again before he spoke.

"I don't know a cop who does it for the money. Same as a soldier. I only met a damn few who were there for the killing. You're trained. You do a job."

"Yes, but you have to elect to do the job. Where does a decision like that come from? I guess it must be the heart. The soul. The brain would tell you it didn't make any sense."

"Somebody has to do it. Somebody has to flip the hamburgers, somebody has to pick up the trash. Somebody has to head big corporations, and somebody has to type the letters. Amazingly enough, it all balances out."

She had never thought of it that way before. He was right. "You put your life on the line every day. Were there times when you wanted to flip the burgers?"

"No. My reactions to life are too intense, I guess. I have to make that difference. I'm good at what I do. It's curious . . . I learned one thing about myself in combat." He paused, and Sterling was very careful not to breathe or move lest his thoughts be diverted.

"When you're calm, you do your job. When you're mad, you want to hurt someone. When you're scared, you want to kill. I was scared a lot in Vietnam. That's why I was good at what I did. I've been scared as a cop. That's just the way it is. It's the way I am. It's me."

She tightened her hold on his hand. "Is that the way you are, Joe? Right now. Scared?"

It broke the ambiance. She almost knew it would before the words were off her lips, but she wanted to know the answer. She wanted him to know the answer. It was such a sweet gesture, taking her hand. Did he realize? She held his hand even tighter and motioned for him to remain lying there. She knew he wanted to get up, but then this talk would be over.

"Joe?" she coaxed him gently.

"I guess it could be described as scared. Angry. Sad. Lost. Shocked. Disappointed in myself. Generally ticked off. I have come across something, the first something that I can't handle. I don't know what to do."

"What would Red do, if things were reversed?" She kept her eyes closed tight. If she opened them tears would slide down and she knew he didn't want that. What he wanted was important to her. Very important.

Joe grunted. "I don't know. Red was different from me. He was more like you. Always laughing and cutting up. I don't take things any more seriously than they deserve, and generally that's not serious at all, but Red, he . . . had a lightness about him. Things bother me till I set them right. I thrive on challenges. Red, he didn't like challenges. Things weren't right, that was okay with him unless it had an adverse effect and had to be corrected."

"You two made good partners. Balance."

He took his hand from hers then and slid over to rest his back against the rock. She heard him opening the picnic basket.

"Conversation over for now, huh?" she concluded, wanting the special feeling his touch gave her.

"For now. I wouldn't want you to accuse me of starving you, and the Miracle Whip might spoil on your peanut butter sandwich."

She laughed then. "I know you have to be kidding, but

I do love that. Seriously, with Fritos crushed up all over."
She opened one eye and looked up at him, shading her
face from the sun.

He was smiling down at her, shaking his head. Nothing
about this woman could be as it appeared. Absolutely
nothing.

EIGHT

"Besides, conversation would lead me to giving you the third degree," he continued. "That's the only reason I brought you out here. It was to get to the truth. But . . ." He laid foil-wrapped sandwiches on the plates and pulled a bag of chips out of the basket, "I already know you were sent here by somebody to do a job. There's some reason why you're here, Sterling. Maybe I don't want to know just yet. Are you going to eat or just lie there and tempt me to kiss you?"

She didn't move. A sly smile parted her lips and he watched as she slowly sat up. "You bought me a boogie board so you could tempt me out here and question me? Yep, that sure is a cop thing, Joe." She had to laugh a little. "You're different from any man I've ever known. One minute you're so sure of everything and then the next you're sure of nothing. Did it ever occur to you, even once, that you might be wrong?"

He peeled the foil from the wine and popped the cork. "Stuff's warm. And no, I'm never wrong."

She fished around and found a glass. Holding it up for him to fill, she stated flatly, "Yes. Yes, you are. You came here like a wounded elephant heads for the graveyard. That was wrong. I won't let you just lie down and wait until your bones are bleached."

He filled both glasses. "You won't let me? That's an interesting statement. A little snip of a woman like you couldn't prevent me from doing anything."

"I didn't mean it as a physical challenge, Joe. Besides, it doesn't fit the character of the man that unfolds before me. You just need time."

"Time. I'm glad to hear that's all I need. I'm really relieved to hear the answer to all this stated so simply." His tone wasn't entirely pleasant. There was a resentment lurking there.

"You're too valuable a person to just cease to exist. I like you, Joe." She held her wineglass up for a toast. "Here's to friends."

He considered her comment and wondered. He hadn't had many. Hadn't needed them. Hadn't wanted them. Hadn't taken the time to make them. He raised his glass and touched the rim to hers.

After a leisurely lunch, they got back into the water. Conversation danced around nothing and everything. She even managed to get him to laugh a few times.

"You're turning red," he observed as they floated across from each other on the board.

She ran her fingertips along her arm and winced. "We're both going to be sore later. We ought to think about going back."

"I am thinking about it. That movie you wanted me to see the other night . . . ?"

"That stupid romantic one?"

He nodded. "We'll watch it tonight. It's supposed to cool off later, so we'll have a fire and pop some corn and just be lazy."

"That sounds wonderful." And it did. "It's supposed to storm off and on for the next few days. Maybe we should stock up on films and food and dig in for the duration."

He winked at her, and Sterling felt her blood pulse forward. "I think you've changed your strategy. You're going to kill me with kindness in hope that I confess to being a nasty reporter who's decided not to do a story, or a spy for IAD who's decided to turn in a very favorable report on you. I could do with some kindness." She moved closer to him and rubbed his mouth with hers. He had used more complete sentences with her today than in the days they had known each other. She sensed he was beginning to concentrate on other things besides Red. He was beginning to remember that he was a living, breathing member of the human race, like it or not.

"How will you do with aggression?" he asked, lazily, amused.

"Test me," she challenged with a smile on her lips.

He cupped the back of her head with his hand and brought their mouths together. It was as she remembered. Tropical. Sultry. He tasted of salt and sun with a trace of wine. Blazing. Fiery. Those hard, unsmiling lips played with hers. Tasting, teasing. She returned the pleasure. The almost-naked play of his body against hers sent a liquid heat pouring through her entire body. They were alone in a world of their own creation. She wanted it to stay that way for a while, just a little while. The waves beat around them, gulls swooped through the sky.

All she knew was the feel of him, the taste of him, the sound of his moan mingling with hers. How had she lived her life for so long without this man? This stranger that she hadn't even known existed until now. Until now.

He could lose himself with her. He felt it. She made him forget—when she was near him, babbling, or when she was touching him, softly. He knew only her. Was he holding onto her because of the relief she gave him, or was it more? How could he know? Was it possible that he had never really been in love before? He knew he didn't believe in love at first sight and all that romantic rhetoric. He knew himself well enough to understand he'd never looked for love. He never thought it was what made the world go round or what started wars and all the other hype he had heard. But he wondered what it would be like . . . to have someone . . .

But now, here she was. He had looked around often enough and seen couples. Everyone was part of a pair. Riding in cars, having dinner in a sidewalk café, strolling along, fishing, shopping, bowling. Where was his other half? Where was the woman who would share his life with him . . . the one he knew had to be somewhere. He had laughed at himself and dismissed the thoughts as not worthy of the time it took to think about it. And he had opened his black book and called a phone number. One that would provide good dinner company or that would enjoy a night of drinking and dancing in a country-western bar. And any other thing that might happen.

He didn't want to involve her with his life if he was only using her as a diversion from his pain. It wasn't his style. It wasn't him, but then he hadn't been himself since that day. . . .

Reluctantly, he broke the kiss. She still had her eyes closed. She rested her cheek on her arm before she opened her eyes and smiled at him trustingly. "How'd I do?"

"You can handle aggression," he answered huskily. There was a sweetness in her, a gentleness that mixed with the zaniness, and a free-spirited facade that she wanted the world to see. She had opened a window to her soul just for him. Dare he take a long look? Could he risk wanting what he saw? Wanting it to the point of forgetting all else?

He leaned over and kissed her cheek. She curled her arms around his neck, and with that movement, lost their balance on the boogie board. It flipped out from under them and they both fell under the water.

*   *   *

Later that evening, both sunburned and tired, they sat in the middle of the living room on the soft multicolored braided rug and watched *Key Largo*. Flames crackled from the old fireplace casting the room in contented peace.

Stiffening, Sterling got up to stretch out on the sofa. He remained on the floor with his back against it. She studied him. This was all so domestic. They had known each other for such a short time and yet it was as if they were old friends. Their souls had seemed to intertwine from the beginning, despite what went on on the surface.

Was she ready for this? she asked herself as she fought to keep from reaching out and running her hand through his hair, down his neck to his shoulder. The answer came effortlessly. Oh, yes, she'd been alone too long and hadn't even noticed.

She glanced at the TV and back to Joe again. Sterling realized she had been on a mission for the last five years. Two missions actually. One was for Ramsburg. The other was for Sterling Powell. *Don't stop. Don't stop long enough to realize how much you miss your husband and son. Don't stop long enough to let the blame you placed on yourself surface again.* Because she couldn't live with it. The guilt of not stopping them. The charge for not acting upon her instincts to save her family.

It would have to be a very special man to bring her back to life. It had to be Joe MacDaniels who would tap that part of her that she'd kept hidden. And now that it was tapped, she couldn't stop the flow. No matter what she did.

She watched the flames dance and cast shadows against the walls. She listened to the crackle over the sound of the movie. Sterling felt so comfortable. His rich voice brought her abruptly out of her reverie.

Slightly bored and a little annoyed, Joe commented, "Good special effects for such an old film."

Frustrated, Sterling groaned, "Must you always be so

logical? Can't you feel the love and the growing passion between Bogart and Bacall? The fury of the storm only adds to the depiction of it. Are you just checking for authenticity of the plot or how good the actors are playing the part? What about the story?''

"It's okay." He shrugged. "Not real life, but it's okay."

She did ruffle his hair then. "You pretend you haven't got a soul or a heart, but I know it's there. So don't try to be the tough guy all the time. Yeah, sometimes life stinks. Sometimes it's wonderful."

When she wrapped her arms around his neck, he pulled her from the sofa to his lap. Her simple gesture moved him. One of possession. He held her tightly against his chest while he pretended to watch the movie. Contented, she could feel the steady thump of his heart against hers. She took this time to study the lines of his face. The contour of a nose that had been broken before. The way his lips came together in a line under his mustache. His jaw was square and determined looking. His chin was strong and stubborn. It was a handsome face, etched with life. There was honesty and integrity in his eyes along with the kindness, the gentleness, the vulnerability that he fought so hard to disguise.

He felt her eyes on him, just as he felt the fragility of her otherwise strong body melt against him. Her skin was soft, smooth under his rough, calloused hands. He could sense rather than see that she was smiling up at him. He felt safe. Odd that only a smile could make him feel safe. Warm. Invincible.

She wouldn't hurt him. He knew that now. No matter what job she had been sent to do, she wouldn't hurt him.

Wouldn't she? the voice niggled inside of him again. *How can you be sure?*

Joe shook off the doubts. He wanted to give her a chance. Maybe he needed to. Maybe he was in love with her.

Doubts flooded back, nagging. *And maybe*, the voice said, smugly, *maybe you just think you are. It's safer here than out there without her*.

"What are you thinking about?" she asked drowsily.

"I'm wondering how this is going to end . . . and if it ever will."

She punched him. "It's a good movie. You just have no taste at all." Because she was beginning to want him a little too much, she jumped up. "Go ahead, put your stupid Monty Python movie on. I'll fix the popcorn."

"No salt or butter." Aching a little, he watched her bounce to the kitchen area. "And don't wake those hungry cats."

"Lots of salt and tons of butter. The babies are already awake, but they're not hungry yet." She looked down at them crawling around and over each other in the box.

She watched over her shoulder as he changed video cassettes, then settled himself back on the floor. The ashtray that had sat beside him all night was full. Idly, he stuffed the paper from a newly opened pack of cigarettes into it. He stretched his arm across the seat of the sofa and blew smoke rings toward the TV. The ludicrous sounds that always accompanied Python movies filled the room. *He* filled the room. The very maleness of him, the power and the aura that surrounded him at all times floated around her. Sterling let it fill her, strengthen her, encourage her.

When she came back to him, she had two beers and a huge bowl of greasy, slightly scorched popcorn in her hands. He took the cans from her and patted a place on the floor for her to sit. She handed him the bowl and took his ashtray to the kitchen to dump it. Returning with two napkins and the empty ashtray, she sat down beside him. It was as if they had been sharing life like this for years. It all felt so normal and so good.

Later, she took the empty cans and the empty bowl to the kitchen and brought the box of kittens to him. "I'll fix the bottles. They'll eat now or not at all. I'm getting sleepy.''

When she returned with the trio of miniature bottles, she stopped a distance behind the couch and watched. He had taken all the kittens out and placed them in his lap. One had fallen off his knee and was inching its way toward his foot. Another was nestled in the crook of his elbow. Still another, Elliott, was contentedly licking butter from his hand. Gentleness prevailed in the hands she loved to watch. They were so soothing. With one squeeze he could break the kittens that fit in his palm. Hands that could kill, that *had* killed, calmly nurtured these little lives.

An overwhelming wave of love surged through her. A feeling so strong it terrified her. Drawing a deep breath, she put a smile on her face and joined them. ''You'll make them sick,'' she protested teasingly.

''It'll make them tough. And fatten them up a little.''

She laughed, looking at the three kittens with their decidedly little round tummies. ''You're the one who has to stay up with them all night if they get a stomachache.''

He glared at her then, again with the look. ''I'll be sure to do that.''

Long after the kittens were asleep in their box, snuggled into the folds of their blanket, Joe listened to Sterling's breathing. Sometime during the movie, her head had nodded against his shoulder. He'd lifted his arm and pulled her into the crook of it. The water and the sun had taken their toll, and soon she slept. It was midnight and a cold breeze came through the open glass door. The fire had burned to embers.

If he moved he might wake her. If he didn't, he thought grimly, he might wake her and keep her awake. Pushing the kitten box slowly to the side, he got to his knees and cradled her in his arms. Without jarring her, he stood up and carried her to the bedroom. She stirred, but only to hold tighter around his neck.

He scooted the bedspread down with his bare foot before placing her on the cool sheet. As he arranged one of her arms across her stomach and the other down her side, he noticed the pulse in her wrist. It was slow and rhythmic. It was life. *She* was life. Living, breathing reasons for wanting to live. For wanting to be able to feel good again. For wanting to get up every morning as long as she was there. How had all this happened? He wondered if he could handle admitting he was dependent on someone else. He stood there and looked at her for a long moment. Her dark lashes fanned across very red cheeks. Her hair, disheveled from a full day of not bothering with it, spread across the pillow, soft and curling.

A tight knot formed in his gut. He wasn't free—might never be—to give a lady like her the love she deserved. The emotion she drew from him was still crimped, still reserved. If it was ever let loose . . . He turned and left the room and missed the small hand that came up to reach for him.

Rousing momentarily from sleep, she heard him in the kitchen. He was actually straightening things up. He snapped the lights off and slid the door closed. The empty house grew quiet. Still. She pictured Joe walking back to his cottage carrying the box of sleeping kittens in it. He might even be muttering to them as she had caught him doing once in a while. She smiled and turned to snuggle into the pillow and dream.

"Wake up, sleepyhead."

He opened his eyes to slits to see her standing at the foot of his bed. "I'm going to town and I thought I would help you feed the babies before I left. And see if you wanted anything."

He hadn't slept until sometime near dawn. He knew for sure because he'd seen the faintest gleam of light sneak in through the curtains. Now he was drugged with sleep and wanted to stay that way. "What are you going to town for?" He murmured the question.

"To shop. What else?" She gave him a little shake. "Come on. The babies are crying."

He pulled the pillow over his face. "I'm still tired. They can eat later."

His eyes were dark and shadowed with things that bothered a man in the night. She had seen it, felt it. He needed to sleep now, while he was peaceful.

She shrugged. "I'll feed them. Do you need anything from town?"

"I can't think of anything." His voice was slurred from the pillow.

"Okay." She reached down and removed the pillow long enough to peck a light kiss on his stubbled chin. Replacing the pillow, she went to feed the kittens. Before she left, she peeked back in the bedroom. He was sleeping soundly, one leg on top of the sheet.

He was beginning to think she'd left town when finally, hours later, he heard her car pull to a stop. It amazed him how welcome that sound was. He hadn't realized how much he'd been waiting to hear it. Trying for nonchalance, he strolled out to help her unload her car.

Clouds covered the sky. A breeze had picked up and carried moisture across the landscape. Rain threatened, but the weatherman had promised it wouldn't break until after midnight. That had delighted Sterling. She had big plans for tonight, and she didn't want the rain to spoil them.

As he walked toward her, Joe recalled the casual kiss she had dropped on his chin before she left. It was the mere casualness of it that fractured his feelings, sending currents of warmth and trust across his heart. He knew he was beginning to feel better about himself and everything. Was it only a natural healing process that God installed in everyone, or was it her? A combination of both, he concluded.

"You must have spent a potload of money. I was getting worried." Only when the words came out of his mouth did he realize it was the truth.

"I did, and I had a great time." She tossed him the keys. "There's more in the trunk."

After carrying the bags to the counter, he began to rummage around in the groceries. "Who's going to eat all this stuff?"

Playfully, she smacked his hand away. "*We* are. Tonight. *La grande terrace.*" She pointed to the deck. "This evening shall become one of the best and surely the most elite restaurants in the area. You do like spaghetti, don't you?" Her face was at once filled with excitement and doubt.

"Yes, yes I like it all right. Is there a special occasion I don't know about?" He leaned, relaxed and amused, against the counter.

"Life, Joe. Just life. I love it here and I like you. We're going to have fun." Her voice was bright and animated, but she remembered the uneasy feeling she had had when she'd noticed a car following her again today. It had been in the parking lot when she had come out of the grocery store. Sterling had looked around but had seen no one lurking about. She had gotten the feeling it was the same car that tailed them to Delaware, but she was still at a loss to why anyone would be following her. Shrugging it off as silly, Sterling turned her attention back to Joe.

He held out his hand and she walked over and put hers in it. After a moment, he brought her fingers to his lips and kissed them. "Then we have a date tonight. What time?"

"Seven." The lock of his eyes on hers sent a roll of anticipation through her. "And don't be late. Please." She added the word quickly at his look. She knew he didn't like being ordered around. That hadn't taken long to recognize.

He pulled her to him. Just the feel of his body supporting hers made her sway closer. The roughness of his jeans against the soft cotton of her shorts. The hardness of his muscled chest against her breasts; the coarseness of his hands on the smoothness of his arms; the softness of the kiss he placed in her hair—the sensual combination had her reeling.

Control. She needed control. She was used to diving headlong into whatever she wanted, she now needed to concentrate, to take her time. Sterling eased away, striving for lightness. "Now, scoot, go do whatever it is you did before I came along. I'll see you later."

What he had done before she came along? He didn't think so. Not ever again. If for nothing else, he owed her for that. He pushed away from the counter and left her busying herself with the bags of groceries. He felt a smile curve on his lips as he left. He tried to light a cigarette as he went down the steps of her deck. Stopping to shelter the lighter from the breeze, he looked up and across the ocean.

It was calmer today. It rolled instead of crashed. It caressed the shore instead of pounded. The clouds kept the sun from being overly warm, but he could still feel the effect of it on his face. Was this the same ocean, the same sunlight, the same air that had failed to ease him when he arrived? He shook his head and turned in the direction of his cottage. A good book, outside on the deck. That's what he wanted to do.

An hour later, he heard her moving the furniture from inside to outside but he pretended to be unaware and went into his cottage. He didn't want to spoil the evening that she had evidently thought out so well.

As he fixed himself a vodka martini, he found himself looking around the room. At first he had resented her touch here and there. He resented her coming in here and rearranging things, straightening up. But somehow now it all just seemed so natural. He walked to his closet to check his clothes. He hadn't packed with any sense of logic when he had left D.C. He pushed things aside and back again and decided on his brown cord sport jacket and his khaki pants. He was reminded of years and years ago when he was a kid, preparing for a date. He liked the feeling of freedom. He was grateful to Sterling for gradually lifting him up and out of his depression.

He returned to the living room and stretched out on the sofa. Though he opened the book, he could find no interest in it. Depression. It was such a personal thing. He wasn't completely rid of it yet, but at least she had altered things enough so he felt competent to handle it, to work it through. And now he had a reason to do just that.

Before, it was just him. Before Sterling, he'd been satisfied to just dissolve. And looking back, he didn't like that part of him. Pain did much to the soul. Maybe it was more of a healing process than he realized. Maybe he was too hard on himself. He had always expected more from himself than anyone else had. Accepting that brought some peace.

As he dozed off, the book slid from his hand to the floor. The sound of the phone ringing crept into his consciousness. He'd been in the cottage for a couple of weeks, and the phone had never rung. No one knew where he was . . . it couldn't really be ringing. He shook his head and sat up.

It *was* ringing. He vaguely remembered shoving the phone behind the sofa when he'd arrived. He got up, stubbing his toe on the end table, and looked behind the sofa. Cursing, he found it and stretched to reach it. Pulling the receiver up to his ear, he growled a "yeah."

There was silence from the open line. Silence, but he sensed it was deliberate stillness. Kids playing? A startled wrong number? He shrugged and returned the receiver to the cradle. Then he noticed the newspaper that the phone had been sitting on.

It was dated August 1, 1990. He felt his heartbeat accelerate and blood pound through his head. If someone was trying to be funny, he sincerely hoped they had a death wish. The headline read LT. ACCIDENTALLY KILLS HIS PARTNER. He blinked and opened his eyes again, hoping it wouldn't be there. He had brought no such paper with him.

He took the paper back to the couch and sat down and stared at it. How did it get here? Who put it here, and why? No matter what shape he'd been in, he was positive he hadn't brought it with him. Why would he?

Could a former tenant of the cottage have left it here and this was simply the first time he had seen it? It was, after all, behind the sofa. And he had, after all, simply shoved the phone back there when he arrived. And his first days here were but a blur to him now. Yes, that had to be it. There was no other answer. There had better not be another answer.

He stared a long time at the picture of himself on the front page. He didn't dare read the words. He just looked at himself; the cop. It was almost like gazing at a stranger. A sure, secure foreigner. The man in the picture was whole, was confident, and a little cocky. The eyes were clear. The jaw was set. And there was an eagerness about him. He remembered that man, and missed him.

Going to the trash, he folded the paper and dumped it in the can. Tipping back the martini glass, he drained his drink and set the glass in the sink.

He looked at the phone. What had that been all about? It could have been an innocent wrong number. It could have been almost anything. But somehow he felt it wasn't so simple.

He found his shoes and pulled them on. A good run on the beach. That was what he needed. He couldn't let this set him back. He wouldn't let it spoil Sterling's evening. He couldn't let it spoil *his* evening. Damn. Damn.

NINE

She watched Joe go down the steps and jog off down the beach. That was sweet of him, she thought. She'd been wondering how she could arrange to set everything up on the deck without him seeing. Now she was free to set the table with the lacy tablecloth. Delighted with her choice, she placed the daisy-and-carnation bouquet beside the candle centerpiece in the middle of the table.

She looked up to see his retreating back far up the beach. She would show him. Tonight she would show him that there were too many good things in life, too many ways to be happy to want to let it all go. For every bad side there was a good. For every loss there was a gain. For every reason he could think of to cease to exist, she would show him ten to stick around. A good meal, a few frills, watch the sunset, listen to good music and spend time with someone who cared . . . a small offering, but a sincere one.

She busied herself in the kitchen, stirring and tasting her special spaghetti sauce. The phone rang, startling her into dropping the spoon and splattering sauce all over the stove. It had been so long since she'd heard a phone ring, she'd all but forgotten the sound. Pushing a small pad and a pencil over to the telephone, she picked up the receiver.

"Hello," she said expectantly, grimacing as she surveyed the mess around her.

"Sterling, my dear." The familiar voice jolted her back. "You haven't called me with a progress report, so I thought I'd call and get the scoop."

Automatically, she jotted "progress report" on the pad. "I haven't called, Mr. Ramsburg, because I haven't figured out just what this man needs yet." She was smiling to herself. Oh yes she had. What he needed was Sterling Powell.

"I see." She could hear the smile in his voice. "I guess it might take quite a few weeks with this one, being so close to the ocean and all. Might take a good long while, am I right?"

"Never can tell." She ran the pencil absently through her hair.

"There have been some more stories on this whole business in the newspapers. Have you seen any of them?"

She jotted down "newspapers." "No. Haven't been interested in what's going on in the outside world. You were right. I've needed this rest for a long time. I've made friends with him. He's a nice man, Mr. Ramsburg. You'd like him."

"Would I?"

She changed the subject. "How are you doing?"

"Fine, fine. You might want to take a look at the newspapers. Just a good idea to keep up on the case. It's raining here. How's the weather there?"

"Cloudy and threatening, but it's supposed to hold off till sometime after midnight." It was easier to talk of inconsequential things. "Been warm and nice, though. I have a tan and I learned how to boogie board." She held the receiver in the crook of her neck and picked up a wet cloth to wipe some of the sauce from the floor and counter.

"My word. Boogie board? I won't ask. Well, call when you have something to report." She wrote the words "report next week" on the pad. "If it takes a long time, it's okay, you know. You earned a vacation."

"Thank you, Mr. Ramsburg. I'll call next week." She hung up the receiver, laid the pencil by the pad, and hurried to clean up the mess so she could stir the bubbling concoction in the large pan on the stove. Where was that darn cornbread recipe? Phone call forgotten, Sterling went in search of the recipe that she had found at the market. It was just where she'd left it, pinned to the bulletin board.

At six, Sterling stood on the deck and looked around at her handiwork. She had put the stereo just outside the door and fiddled with the tuning button for half an hour until she'd found a station that played easy listening and lots of it.

The table looked lovely with the flowery centerpiece and the candle enclosed in glass that she would light after the sun went down. The wineglasses stood ready, next to the silverware and the china. Expense account. She thought Mr. R. would approve. Two large urns of flowers sat on either side of the door. She could always use them in her apartment later. She looked up at the sky. The clouds were rolling quickly. She hoped the weatherman would be right or the atmosphere she'd worked so hard to create would be spoiled.

Back inside, she studied her dress again. After a critical debate she decided it was perfect. The food was ready, waiting to be heated up, and everything had turned out beautifully. She checked the lemon meringue pie that was in the refrigerator. Yes, it was thawing right on time. So, she'd cheated with a store-bought one, she couldn't do pies. He would never know.

An hour later Sterling stood at the top of the stairs and watched Joe come toward her. He, too, had dressed carefully. She thought he looked handsome and rugged in his brown cord sport coat. Under it, he wore a lightweight sweater, and khaki slacks hugged his thighs. And he wore his boots. She liked it when he wore his boots. They added just the right touch of cocky cowboy.

Joe's nerves stretched as he drew closer. She was a vision for any man's eyes. The dress she wore draped to the tops of her toes. It was blindingly white. A simple white cotton dress with an off-the-shoulder top, cinched at the waist with a narrow leather belt. Its skirt fell into ruffles around the bottom. Three rows for a hint of sass.

Together, they looked as if they were going to a country-western dance for a few quick swings and doe-si-doe's. She had even tugged on white western boots with a silver chain and concho about the ankle.

Had she shopped just to please him? Her hair was loose and full and shiny. It fell in soft curls around her face, tumbled over her shoulders. At her throat she wore a simple single strand of gold. The rubies at her ears winked at him. She smelled of something wonderful. Earthy and sweet. Irresistible.

In a gesture as natural as breathing, she held her hand out to him. "Right this way, sir. Your table has been reserved and your meal awaits you."

He took her hand and pressed it to his lips. When he was able to speak, he spaced the words slowly. "You are beautiful."

She'd been certain she was beyond blushing, but she felt the rush of heat on her cheeks. He was smooth-shaven and she picked up the spicy scent of his cologne.

He glanced around at all she'd done, wondering why she would go to all this trouble for him. And why it made him feel so tense and insecure.

"Do you like it?" she asked, looking around with him.

"What's not to like? It's perfect." He took the seat she indicated while she retreated to the kitchen for the salad.

"I saw you go for a run on the beach earlier . . ." she began. "I would have liked to have joined you, but I was too busy. Maybe tomorrow." She chatted idly as she arranged bowls and dressing on the table.

"If it's not raining," he agreed flatly.

Sterling wasn't at all pleased with his mood. They had had such a nice, comfortable evening with each other the night before, and now he seemed to be on edge about something. Had she overdone it?

He ate his salad silently. It was good, but his mind was dragged back to the phone call. He nodded when she asked him a question that he only half heard. And the newspaper bothered him more than he was willing to admit. Before coming over here, Joe had gone to the trash can and forced himself not to get it out and read it. He toyed with a carrot stick. How had they colored the story? Had they let the world know for how many years and just how closely he and Red had worked together? Damn it, they'd been like brothers. How could that kind of intimacy be written in black and white. Or did they make it seem like he was a rookie cop who'd made a stupid mistake? Did he really want to know?

"You're awfully quiet, Joe. Is anything wrong?"

She was looking at him with such concern in her eyes. He didn't want to spoil this evening and even more, he didn't want to share the tug-of-war of pain and doubt waging inside him. "No. I'm just down tonight. I'll get over it."

"I know you don't like me to worry about you, Joe. I do, though. If there's anything I can do to help, I will."

He smiled up at her, but there was an edge of irritation in his voice. "Don't you think I know that by now? And I wouldn't be down if I could help it."

Salads done, she brought the spaghetti and was a little disappointed when he didn't even comment on it. He did clean his plate, though.

She cleared the table after dinner was done, except for the centerpiece, the wine, and a nice big ashtray she had bought for him that afternoon. Because she wanted this evening to be a pampering one, she declined his offer of help. In Sterling's philosophy, everybody needed to be spoiled once in a while.

The sun was almost down, the clouds tipped dark. The breeze kicked up, whipping at the large deck. Sterling sighed inwardly. She didn't want to think of moving things inside. Not just yet. She eyed the sky warily and hoped.

A slow love song wafted on the air. She slipped her boots off and pushed them under the table. On impulse, she stood up and went around to his chair. "May I have this dance, sir?"

He looked up at her. She was so lovely. And either so innocent or so good at pretending. Whichever, a dance sounded good to him.

She went gently into his arms. She again felt the power that surrounded him, the strength in his body. He exuded a pure male sexuality that was undeniably potent at this range. Wanting to lean into him, to feel his entire body with hers, she kept the small distance between them and ventured a look at his face.

He hadn't come close to preparing himself for it. The power this woman had over him. He caught her light scent and felt the soft weight of her hand on his shoulder.

He was gazing down at her. There was no smile on his lips, none in his eyes, but his hold was gentle. As if he were afraid to break her. They swayed together naturally, the breeze ruffling her skirts around her ankles as she moved.

Joe was grateful he still had such control. He wanted to take her to his bed now. Right now. Feelings for her flowed from him that were more than simple biological responses. He wanted to be the recipient of the love she so clearly had to give. He wanted to release the love and respect that he knew was beginning to swirl around inside him. She was made for him. She would melt against a man's body. His body. She would become part of him. It at once scared and pleased him. He wondered if she made love with as much passion as she lived every day.

He wanted to touch and be touched by the goodness in her. God, he needed that. The goodness, the genuineness that he trusted was there. If he could only let himself go, he could love her, really love her. It would comfort him so much to know that she would always be there. But a man like him didn't like the word comfort. Share, blend, he decided. Better words. He had never had anyone who simply did those things. He didn't know how she felt. She seemed to care quite a bit about his solace, his happiness, but it could just be her way. It might be best for both of them if he let himself believe that.

She closed the gap between them and laid her head on his chest. The move, so simple, so natural, had his stomach clenching.

She couldn't help herself. He was so strong. So solid. So male. It both intrigued and frustrated her. He was all reserve again, on the alert. She had to get him to relax or this whole evening would be a waste. And then the love song conjured up new waves of contentment that seemed to ebb and flow from her toward him. It wasn't something she could stop, so she enjoyed it.

The breeze played around them as the song went from one beautiful recording to another. Joe was almost unaware when he brushed his lips against her hair. She moved so that he made contact with her forehead.

They were no longer taking actual steps, just standing close, swaying together. She could feel her pulse speeding up and the answering sound of his heartbeat increase in tempo beneath her ear.

"Joe." His name was a sigh. "You dance wonderfully. Did you have a lot of girlfriends before all this happened? One special one?"

"No. I was married for a while. A long time ago. She liked to dance."

"What happened?"

He moved his shoulders restlessly. "She couldn't put up with my job. Some women can't handle the constant chance that things could be over in a second."

"She must have loved you very much."

His voice was cold and unforgiving. "No. She didn't love me enough." He avoided looking at Sterling.

"You still miss her?" she ventured, needing to know.

"It was a long time ago, Sterling. A long time ago. I don't know how I feel about her anymore. I don't think about it. What's over is over, and that's that."

When the song ended, they separated a little, but he continued to hold her hand. It was nearly dark now, and dampness had intensified the aroma of the flowers decorating the deck. The breeze continued to play over Joe and Sterling as the gulls swooped and raced nearby to finish their evening meal.

A last ray of sunlight caught the sliver of gold that lay around her neck. Needing to taste, needing *her*, he bent his head to lay a kiss there.

Warmth burst through her that splayed its way in all directions. She slid her hand from his shoulder up into his hair. Seduced by the flavor, he trailed his lips up her neck, across her cheek, and lingered there momentarily. A whisper's breath away from her mouth. Opening her eyes, she stared at her own reflection in his.

He rubbed his lips across hers, lightly, hovering, now not moving . . . only tasting, testing. Her lips parted, waiting, attending, permitting.

He kissed her shoulder that her dress left bare, then her neck just below her ear. Then his mouth trailed lightly, slowly, across her face. Still tasting, he pressed a kiss beneath her jaw.

She wanted to pull him close to her, mold herself against him, but he kept her just there, not moving, with nothing touching but their lips and hands.

She trembled with the anticipation of a kiss. Again, his kiss made her wait, as he only slid his mouth across hers, ever so easily. He left her lips hungry to take his down the hollow of her throat. She was floating, drifting. She was thistledown on the wind; she was a bubble floating away.

Wanting more, she pulled her hands from his to draw him close. His head came up and she closed the space between them frantically. A low moan from both of them mingled as mouth closed on mouth.

He banded her waist with his arms and picked her up off the deck so that their faces were level without breaking the kiss. She dipped her hands in his hair at the back of his neck and felt the soft coarseness of it. She reveled in the feel of his hard body against hers, trembled at the power of it while he swayed slowly, in time to the music.

He broke the kiss and looked at her with dark, smoky eyes. Everything he wanted was in his arms. A smile played at the corners of his mouth as he trailed short, sensuous kisses along her jaw, back to her lips.

She let her tongue play with his mouth, taste him, savor him. When she changed the angle of the light kiss, she felt him tremble with it.

Slowly, so slowly that she felt every line, every muscle of his body, he set her on her feet. She felt the wooden planks dip under her and held tight to him for balance. He put his fingers under her chin and tilted her head so he could look into her eyes.

These kisses were not like the ones he had taken from her before. These were to seduce, to draw nectar, to tease, to ask. Music forgotten, they moved to their own tune as the depth of their connections grew. Falling. Sliding. Tumbling. She clung to him, wrapping her arms around him. With every move she gave him the permission he silently asked.

Hovering, she was no longer in contact with the real world. Slipping, floating somewhere dark and far away, but with him. Only him. Melting. Nothing else existed but the feel of him, the taste of him. The promise of him.

He had sensed there was passion in her, but he hadn't come close to the power of it. She came to him so willingly, so openly, so trustingly. But could she be trusted? He didn't want to think; he didn't want the answer. He only knew what it felt like to get lost in this woman. To lose control of all thought, relinquish regulation to instinct. He groaned as she trembled and sighed beneath his hands.

She knew his gentleness was the result of great restraint. She could feel the deepening intimacy each time he returned his roving mouth to her lips and, with that restraint, she became impatient, avid. She didn't want him to feel the need for suppression. She wanted him turned loose. Hunger ripped through her and she locked herself against him.

With whisperlike movements his mouth roamed her jaw, her throat, her shoulder. Answering, she turned her mouth to his temple, to his cheek.

He heard as he felt her quickened breath at his ear. Joe knew the soft moistness of her mouth as it played with him, stirred him, fired him.

Spiraling and dizzy, she held tight around his neck when he scooped her up and walked inside and toward the bedroom. In the light of day she had seen him as a man who did things quickly with marked results. In the darkness she began to know him as a man who did things slowly, savoringly. The hands that could kill, the hands that could decide life or death, held here, drew fire from deep within her. And asked.

She answered. The rain splatted against the windows, pattered against the rough boards of the deck. Thunder rolled in the distance. Lightning flashed, echoing her passion.

"The radio and the silk flowers will get wet," she murmured against his mouth.

"Let them. Nothing matters but us. Nothing exists but us." He set her feet on the floor. The wind increased and shuddered through the cottage. In the dim light he searched her face as he framed it between his hands. What he saw in her eyes, in the way she held on to him, was what he'd hoped to see. What he needed to see.

She slid his jacket off his shoulders. He undid the belt at her waist. She helped him slip the sweater over his head. He watched as the dress floated down her hips into a puddle on the floor. Soon, flesh to flesh, her moan of pleasure mingled with his as he laid her back on the bed, gently, slowly. He wanted to remember for all time the way she looked at him tonight. She lifted her arms up toward him. Holding back only long enough to cherish the anticipation, to revel in her eagerness, Joe bent down to her.

Her small hands smoothed over his body, trailing fire, drawing beads of moisture to his skin.

The tips of her breasts blossomed under his hands. She shuddered as he moved one hand and replaced it with his mouth. He nipped, he let his tongue trail over, then back again. He suckled.

Sterling dove her hands into his hair, then trailed her fingers down and across his broad shoulders. She never wanted him to move, to put space between them again. His muscles were hard and flowing beneath her palms. She wanted him. Wanted him now.

He made her wait. Made himself wait. If he took her now, it would be fast and furious. She deserved better than that. He took her hand and guided it down, over his chest, his flat stomach, and down. He heard her gasp as she found him. Her fingers curled around him.

She turned to her side and pressed a kiss to his shoulder. Her mouth trailed to his stomach and lower. She heard his moan of rapture and it pleased her. She wanted to make him happy. She wanted him to forget everything except her. She wanted to be the reason he couldn't get his breath. Demanded that he know how very much she loved him.

They rolled together across the bed, the sheets becoming twisted and lost.

Gently, he pushed her away from him to blaze a path of fire with his mouth. His tongue darted down the side of her breast, her waist, over her hip.

She didn't want to wait any longer. Couldn't. Sterling whispered his name and brought his face back to hers. There was something different in his eyes. Not just the passion that brought beads of perspiration to his forehead, though it had his eyes dark and sleepy; there was a reverence, a sweetness, and a vulnerability she had never seen before.

He moved until he was poised over her. She accepted his full body weight with a low sigh and opened for him. Instantly, and then slowly, she was filled with him as he slipped inside her. Nerves that had been forced to the edge of her skin became so alive that she was aware of every sensation possible. She heard his moan, felt his body shudder with the contact. His mouth softened on hers, then became ardent and guiding.

He pushed her further, drew her back to him, and then led her along the path of a new world, one of heat and dark, of colors and cooling, one of sparks and fire. "Sterling," he whispered.

She wrapped her arms and legs around him and gave him what he needed, what *she* needed.

He wasn't going to hurry. He wasn't going to let the tempo take him. And then he no longer had a choice. It built in him quickly, savagely. As she rose to meet him, stroke for stroke, as she arched toward him and dipped her tongue into his mouth, to taste, to explore, he went with her into the haze and heat. As she said his name against his lips, he took her over the edge, locked together, giving and receiving.

She awoke to the small stream of light wafting through the slit in the curtains. She didn't want to move. Didn't want to risk disturbing him. It felt so right to wake up with his arm pinning her against his chest. She heard the light, even thud of his heart and smiled when she remembered the sound of it pounding double time during the night. Her left leg was lodged beneath his. The sheets were twisted and coiled around them. A cool breeze coming in from the deck door chilled her. She snuggled closer to him.

His hand came off her shoulder and brushed her hair back. "I thought you were going to sleep the day away."

The sound of his deep, rumbly voice excited her. Just the gentle touch of his hand made her want. "It's only daybreak," she remarked as she tilted her head so she could look at him.

He smiled. A bright and wonderful smile. "I don't like wasting any time I have with you, Sterling. You're more beautiful right at this moment than I have ever seen you." His finger traced her lips. She nipped at him. Taking his hand between both of hers, Sterling uncurled his fingers and ran her tongue across his palm. For now, right now, those hands that she admired so much belonged just to her. She kissed his knuckles, held the back of his hand to her cheek. In his work, they were quick to react to decisions and, with her, they were sure at getting reactions.

"I suppose you don't remember a thing that happened last night. The spaghetti, you didn't even say it was good."

"The best. I didn't think I had to tell you." His hair was tousled and falling across his forehead. She brushed it back.

He took her hand and brought it to his mouth reveling in her instant response. She leaned close and brushed her lips across his cheek, catching the night's growth of beard and enjoying the soft, sensual caress of his mustache. He turned his lips to meet hers.

"You don't have to tell me anything, Joe." She nuzzled

his neck, tasted his shoulder. Her mouth roamed over his chest.

"How about if I tell you to be quiet?" he asked softly. "You talk too much. I want more action."

She smiled as he turned on his side and cradled her. Lifting her mouth eagerly to his, she teased; "Action, huh. You asked for it." She pulled the sheet away and threw it on the floor. Sterling reached for him and he grabbed her hands, bringing her hard against him.

When she awakened this time, it was to the smell of bacon and eggs. She glanced at the clock on the nightstand. Noon. She opened her eyes wider. Noon! And she didn't have bacon and eggs in the house. Pulling the sheet loosely around her, she padded into the kitchen.

He was dressed in jeans and a T-shirt that advertised he-man drinking habits. He had sneakers on and his hair was combed neatly. He had dressed and gone to the store. As he stirred what she knew would be a terrible mess of scrambled eggs, her heart nearly gave way. She was in love with this man. There was no more question. No more doubt. No more wondering. As she stood there watching his movements about the kitchen, he turned and saw her, towel-wrapped frying pan handle in his grip and a warm smile just for her.

He glowered at her lazily. "If you don't want all my efforts to prepare your breakfast to go for nothing, don't stand there in that sheet and look at me like that." He moved toward her.

He was so sure, so cocky. She walked to him and opened the sheet and cocooned him inside with her. He swiveled to set the pan back on the stove. Turning the knob, the flame under the burner died.

He held her an arm's length away. Grinning, his gaze swept down and then up. She pulled his T-shirt up and placed a kiss on his chest. Yanking the shirt over his head, she pulled him closer and kissed him just above the snap on his jeans.

Joe took the sheet from her, wanting nothing between them. The need to be in her arms was overwhelming. He allowed it to guide him. He picked her up, the sheet trailing to the floor, as he carried her back to bed. He was happy. More than that. He was at peace.

"You were right. It tastes the same heated or freshly cooked—terrible." He pushed his plate away.

She nibbled a piece of cold bacon and shoved the rubbery eggs around on her plate. "The toast and the bacon are perfect. You're perfect, Joe."

Her words touched his heart, made it jerk in his chest. He smiled at her. Sometime during the night, and now, his life had changed. Where it had been dark and uncertain before, it was now bright and sure. As quickly as it had become destroyed on the night he shot Red, it began its road to reconstruction. He wanted to tell her what she had done for him, but words would never be enough. He took the plates and set them in the sink. When he turned around he did a double take. "What the hell are those for?"

"They're called kites, Joe. Always after a rainy night, there is a good rush of wind. Ready?" She took a step toward him, one bright kite in each hand, their tails trailing on the floor.

He left the sink and swept her up in his arms and round and round, tripping over the knotted tail. "I'm ready, Sterling. Let's go fly your dumb kites. Why not?"

She laughed and tried to regain her balance. "Set me down before we both fall."

He looked deep into her eyes and lowered his mouth to kiss her smiling lips. "Would it be so bad if we both fell?"

"No." She rubbed her mouth against his. "Unless we broke something and ended up in one cast and unable to move." She teased him, tracing his mouth with her tongue.

He set her down gently and took her face between his hands. She stood there, her arms outstretched, holding the kites. She could tell he wanted to say something. Deep down, where feelings begin their journey to become words, something stirred in him. She could see it in his eyes, feel it in his touch. Time. Time and her love. He needed both. And she would give it to him. That and more. Everything she had was his.

He planted a kiss on top of her nose. "Bet my kite goes higher than yours. You don't know who you're playing with, little girl."

She shook her head as he followed her out onto the deck. "Nope. Not possible. My ball of string is longer than yours. I'm not stupid. I already thought of that."

"That's cheating." he swatted her playfully.

She cast him a sly smile over her shoulder and all but danced down the deck stairs onto the warming sand. "You got that right, cop. It is definitely fraud. Isn't that a felony? How many years would I have to serve for that?"

He kissed the back of her neck. "However many you want." Then, jerking the kite out of her right hand, he started running down the beach, kicking sand behind him. The kite took to the air and began its ascent.

"Hey, no fair. You got the one with the longer string. That's mine." She ran down the beach after him, her heart about two feet out in front of her. She had never been so happy.

As she tried to get her kite to take flight, she kept her eyes on him. He was her whole life. From now on, from this time on, he would belong to her. They would have a family someday . . . She looked back as her kite caught on the breeze and lifted. She gave it slack and at the same time let her imagination wander. Yes, they could share the years to come, but for right now, this was enough.

"Look out, MacDaniels. Our strings will get tangled.

You're such a show-off." *And once you tangle with me,* she thought smugly, *you'll never get loose.*

A solitary figure stood behind the front angle of the cottage and watched as Joe and Sterling scampered down the beach. From under the watcher's feet, grains of sand shifted slowly down the hill.

TEN

They played like children on the beach. Sterling flew her kite until her arms ached. Finally, she ran to the deck and tied the string around the railing, admiration shining in her eyes as she watched Joe.

He was grinning up into the sky as he watched his kite respond to his maneuvering. It dipped, it soared, it looped at his command. Right now, at this moment, his mind was cleared of his haunts. He was as free as the balsa wood and plastic that flew overhead. *This is as it should be*, Sterling thought.

The kite fluttered and dropped erratically. He saved it at the last moment with a good flick of his wrist, and it soared, straining wildly against the thin length of string. Sterling heard his laugh travel on the breeze. She propped her chin in her hand and leaned against the railing. She cursed herself for not bringing a camera. Fighting a sudden uneasiness in her mind, she prayed she never had to depend on pictures for memories.

He looked up and saw her watching him. "Hey, lazy, that's a cop out."

"That it is. I'm fine. I'm enjoying watching you." And she was. She was content for the first time in years. Really content and feeling competent to handle anything that came up. Being with Joe had opened doors she hadn't realized she had closed. Being with him had awakened her from a self-imposed deep sleep. She could never close her eyes again.

Joe took his kite to his own deck and tied it there. The two kites flew over the top of the cottages and hovered on the brink of crashing. He jogged down the steps and she came down hers to meet him.

They ran ankle-deep in the water, splashing each other. Laughing, they waded out farther, where he proceeded to dunk her. When she came up, he lifted her over his head and swirled her around and then dunked her again.

Spitting and sucking in air, Sterling rammed him, pushing him under the water and holding him there. He grabbed her ankles and pulled them out from under her. Both under the water, he pulled her to him and they bounced to the top.

"I give up," she surrendered breathlessly, holding her hands up high in the air. "I know you're stronger than I am. I admit it." Then with a devilish smile on her lips, she pushed for him again, laughing. "But I'm faster."

Body rubbed body, hands held hands, mouth found mouth. They laughed, they teased, they held, and they enjoyed each other. She leaned into him and he let her. He held her gently so that they floated on the waves.

Later that afternoon, they found a faded, warped Frisbee under his deck and they chased that around for a while. When they'd exhausted each other, they collapsed on the lower steps of her deck. She leaned her tired body against him, her cheek resting on his arm. Content, he kissed the top of her head.

"I want to cut my kite loose."

"What? Why? Then you can't run it again."

"You want to let yours go?" She rubbed her face against the warm strength of his body and sighed.

"Not really. I sort of enjoyed that. Dumb as it is."

She laughed but didn't move. She was too comfortable. Too aware of the swell of feelings the two of them were enveloped in.

"Well . . ." she jumped up a few moments later, and went up the stairs. "I'm going to. They're cheap. I'll buy another one if I want it."

He got up and followed her to the deck and waited while she tried to undo the knot. Giving up, she went inside and came back out with a knife.

She looked up at him. "Ready?"

He nodded and watched the expression on her face instead of the kite as she cut through the string. Her smile turned into a sigh as she watched the kite rise quickly and flutter to a point where it was only a spot in the sky.

"I don't understand you," he confessed as he pushed curls from her neck.

"What?" She turned and gave him a kiss.

"You enjoyed the hell out of that kite and now you just let it go. Why?"

"I don't know. I wanted to see what it looked like. I wanted to see it go from total freedom to imminent destruction."

"Even if that meant you could never have it again?"

She shrugged. "I guess so. It was great while it lasted. Anyway," she smiled up at him, "we still have yours."

He banded her with his arms and held her close. Her chin rested on his chest, head tilted so she could study him. It scared her when she really thought about all this. He was so beyond anything, any man she had ever known. He was more than real life. He was everything life should be.

He looked down at her and ran his finger along her cheekbone. "Yes, we still have mine. Sterling . . . ?"

She saw the laughter go out of his eyes. She felt the

way his body tensed and steered him off course immediately. "If you're going to get serious, don't, please. Not now. Later. Later we'll talk, but now, just for now, just hold me."

He lowered his mouth to hers slowly, inch by inch, and then with a fury that caught him off guard, he kissed her, drawing her very soul to meet his.

How could this be? she asked herself as she let her tongue roam to meet with his. How could all this be so different from anything she had ever known? How had she lived the last five years without him?

Later, they carried wood to the shoreline and built a fire. The sun went down, slowly, sketching beautiful pictures as it went. Clearly defined streaks of red, orange, gray, and pink melted into rainbow sherbert. He held her hand and smiled at her reactions to the changing colors. He would never be able to watch another sunset without remembering this moment. The air chilled as the sky darkened and the last ray of sunlight faded below the horizon.

"What are you thinking about, Sterling?" He wondered if her thoughts followed the same path as his. Was she capturing this moment with her heart?

Sterling was wrapped in a blanket and sitting Indian-style next to Joe and watched as he held a stick with a marshmallow on it over the flames.

"When I was a little girl, my sister and I used to stay up after lights-out and compare our dreams of Prince Charming. We'd giggle and talk until Mom or Dad would come in and tell us to quiet down."

"That stopped you?"

"For a few minutes, then most of the time we would start again."

"What did your Prince Charming look like?"

"Smooth. Tall, blond, blue eyes." Sterling stared into the crackling flames as she recalled.

"I see." He pretended to be wounded and tested the consistency of the marshmallow with a finger.

She leaned on his shoulder. "Children often have no grasp of reality. Sometimes I used to wonder if I would be cursed with that forever." The water rolled close to her bare toes.

He heard a tone in her voice he hadn't caught before. Wistfulness? He really didn't know much about her. "You sound as if you had a good childhood. You mentioned a brother. How many kids were in your family?

"Just the three of us. I was lonesome most of the time. Of course that was self-imposed. My brother included me in what he could, but he had boy things to do. My sister was the cute, obedient one. I preferred to do things on my own. Every time I would climb too high in the tree or run off to play in the woods, my sister would run in to tell. After a while I got pretty good at not getting caught. I occupied myself very well."

"Me, too. I was always doing something. I don't remember thinking or dreaming, just doing. I guess it's better that way. Then you don't have to disappoint yourself."

He'd held the marshmallow over the fire too long and it fell off into the cinders. He simply put another one on.

"I'd like to have known you when you were a little boy." And a teenager . . . a soldier in Vietnam . . . a rookie cop . . . and now the narc. She tried to picture him in eight-pocket baggy pants, a brightly colored shirt with cut-off sleeves, and a Willie Nelson headband. "Do you think about those days much?"

"No. Here, this one is just right." He took the gooey white blob and offered it. She opened her mouth and he dropped it on her tongue. She had some of it on her lips and he moved to get it off with his mouth. "Umm. Tastes good."

She fastened her gaze on him. She could never get enough of looking at him. "I wish we could stay here and simply live like this for the rest of our lives. Friends. Comrades. Lovers."

Touched, he put the stick down and cradled her in his arms. "We can stay for as long as you like."

She opened her blanket to envelop him in with her. "I have a job to go back to, and so do you."

She felt him stiffen at once and cursed herself for bringing it up. Was there a future for them together, always, as she was hoping?

"We don't have to talk about it just now," he whispered.

"Okay, Joe." She wanted to say, Do you love me, Joe?, because if he did, all the answers were simple. But it was her pride—and her fear that the answer would be no—that kept her silent. She was afraid that even if he did love her, he wouldn't see it for that. She wondered how he *did* see things.

But he was right. For now, just for now, the whole world could go on spinning without them. She found his mouth and kissed him. Soon they lay back on the sand and held each other, listening to the sounds of the fire crackling and the ocean advancing and retreating. Reality was only for those who chose to recognize it as such, and for now, she refused.

That night, lying next to him in her bed, curled up and molded against him from head to toe, Sterling listened to his breathing. He was her knight in shining armor. He was the only thing that mattered to her.

How quickly life could change, she marveled, and shifted a little as he did. She could feel the beat of his heart where her hand lay. A while ago it was wild, and now it was restful. An hour ago his body was sheened with perspiration and pulsing with life. His hands and his mouth had brought her feelings and emotions to full stand. It was nearly morning and she couldn't sleep even though she was exhausted. She was afraid that if she closed her eyes, it would all be gone when she awoke.

Browning. 9mm Automatic. Cold, heavy steel. The hand wrapped around the gun squeezes the trigger, feels the jar as the bullet fires. Flash of fire. Stench of sulfur.

Slow speed, the spiraling lead makes its way toward its target. Shock. Realization. Terror. Blood stops pumping through his veins. His heart is still. The target is Red. And he is the shooter.

Get the bullet. Stop it! But his feet are too heavy and his legs won't respond to the message his brain is sending his muscles. His arms are outstretched, fingers clawing the air trying to reach it. His mouth is open but no sound comes out.

No air. His lungs are locked. He gulps for air. Stubbornly, the bullet makes its way, inch by inch, toward the other man. This can't be! He tries to move, but something stops him. Something slows him down, pulls him backward. He strains to shout his friend's name, opens his mouth, forces air toward his lips, but nothing.

Red's surprised expression becomes clear in the darkness. He is looking right at Joe. Joe can hear his own voice echo in his head as he demands his legs to move, demands the bullet to stop, but it stays right off the end of his fingers. Too late.

Sweat mixes with the smell of fear and becomes sickening. His gut twists with pain as he tries to lift one foot and then the other. *Get to him. Don't let this happen. Red! Red! Move, Red! Don't catch the bullet. I'll get it!* But he couldn't go any faster no matter how hard he strained. Everything remained in an agonizing slow advance.

Thump! Red is slammed back against the wall. Blood oozes from the hole in his chest. Joe feels his own chest being ripped apart. Red looks at Joe, eyes wide. Surprise. Pain. He grabs at his chest. *Here, Joe, here. It hurts here. Help me, Joe.* He slides down the wall, inch by inch.

Slurred speech. More heat. More darkness. The sound of sirens in the distance.

No air to breathe. An anguished cry moves slowly from his lips to arch across the air above him. Not Red! Not Red! Despair. Futility.

Joe finally reaches Red. Red claws for his jacket and holds on. Weight. Falling. Pain-filled eyes close to his, pleading. Joe holds Red and together they slide to the pavement. Blood covers Joe's hands. *Oh, God, not him. Me! Me!* Red's eyes close. He stops breathing. His eyes open, unseeing. Dead. Death. Nothing. Joe struggles for air, struggles to lift Red. Cold air rushes into his lungs. He greedily sucks it in and a cry of agony splits the peaceful darkness.

Sterling was jolted awake, her blood pounding in her head. Joe had gone mad! He was screaming. He'd jumped from the bed and pressed himself against the wall. In the dark, she could see his face, all shadows, was glistening with sweat and tears; he breathed like a man held under water too long. She'd survived enough nightmares to recognize one. She started to get out of bed and go to him when she was stopped by the look on his face and the hand he shot out to stop her.

His chest heaved. He kept his back pressed against the wall. He squeezed his eyes tightly shut and then opened them again. "I'm all right. I'm all right."

With absolute determination, Sterling moved slowly to stand a few feet from the man she loved. "It'll be okay, Joe. It was just a nightmare. It isn't happening again. It's over." She held out her hand to him. "Let me help you."

He shook his head, and staggering away, he disappeared into the bathroom. She felt the coldness of the empty room and hugged her arms around her.

Joe braced himself against the sink and slowly brought his head up to look at his reflection in the mirror. Sweat streamed down his face. His eyes were dark and haunted. His mouth was open and his breathing was ragged. Turning on the faucet, he cupped both hands under the stream of cold water and brought a splash of it across his face and upper body. He hated this. Weakness. What else could it be?

Jerking a towel off the rack, he buried his face in it. He had seen the look of terror in Sterling's eyes. He recognized it buried deep in his own. These were worse nightmares than the ones that stayed with him since Vietnam. He, alone, was responsible in these. There was no rationale. He wasn't surrounded by men who had experienced the same thing. He wasn't one of many men who had a nasty job to do. It was only him and his friend. He threw the towel on the floor and breathed deeply, swearing.

She was still standing there when Joe came out of the bathroom. She watched as he went into the living room and lit a cigarette. Without saying a word, Sterling followed him in, then walked to the refrigerator to pour him a glass of vodka.

Returning, she went up behind him as he slumped before the glass door looking out into the nothingness. She came up to stand beside him and offered him the drink. Steadier now, he put an arm around her shoulder and accepted the glass, sipping the bracing liquid and remaining silent.

"Let's go back to bed," she coaxed him gently.

He shook his head, so she simply stayed there beside him, her arm around his waist.

When he spoke, his voice was thick with emotion. "We'd been on this case for months. Our man dealt drugs and killed cops."

She stood stock-still beside him, her heart tearing at the pull of his strained words.

"The last two weeks, we had staked out and watched and gotten his movements down to the last step. When it went down we called for backup before we went in. Red was supposed to stay with me. He didn't." He drew hard on his cigarette and blew the smoke toward the ceiling with vengeance. Dragging a hand through his hair, he slid the door open and sagged against the frame.

"Somehow, our target got wise to us. He made a break for it. Bullets were flying. We were ducking and then we were chasing him. Red and I were determined this slime wasn't going to get away clean."

She tightened the arm she had around his waist when she felt him sway the slightest bit. A tear rolled silently down her cheek.

"We chased him for blocks, dodging fire from his semi. It was dark except for the occasional lights from inside buildings, and there was this flashing orange neon light." He rolled away from the arm she kept around him and paced the room. "It kept going on and off, steady and rhythmically. I remember that." His breath shuddered and he sipped his drink before continuing. "It was about three in the morning, so no one was out. It was a bad neighborhood, industrial and housing units. If people heard gunfire there once, damn it, they heard it three times a week. They stayed inside, out of danger."

She caught him as he paced by her and put her arms around him. "Don't do this to yourself, Joe."

He shook her off, pivoted, and stalked out onto the deck. Determined, she followed him, eased up behind where he stood at the edge of the deck, and pressed her cheek against his shoulder. Feeling him stiffen at her touch, Sterling told him, "I'm not going anywhere. There's nothing you can do to make me leave you alone." He relaxed a little, the feel of her soft body against his reassuring him. Somehow, knowing that she wouldn't just go away strengthened him.

Long moments later, they walked to the couch. He took her arm from around him and held her hand. They sat beside each other and Sterling put her other hand over their joined ones. It was then he saw the tears on her face. He wiped them away with his fingers and he kissed her lightly.

He took a long drag on his cigarette and blew the smoke toward the floor, weary. He rested his head on the back of the couch "I kept in voice contact with Red most of the time, but we were all moving so fast. Somewhere along the line, I was running alone. A relay of fire came from just inside this building. By this time I was mad and scared and just downright determined this creep was coming down before he killed another cop. I saw him move to slide inside the doorway and I raised my gun, beaded in, and squeezed off."

Fresh tears filled her eyes as she watched the pain pierce across Joe's face.

"So I killed the cop." His voice was lifeless. "I had no way of knowing Red had gotten ahead of us somehow. But it was my responsibility to know, for sure, who I was pulling the trigger on. I killed my friend. I don't remember much after that. There was blood on my hands for a long time. I guess it'll always be there." He stared down at them now.

She raised the hand she held between both her own and kissed it. "It was an accident, Joe. An accident. Everyone knows that. Everyone but you. You have to come to terms with it."

"That easy, is it? I'm glad to hear it. Red had a family, damn it, a wife, kids, brothers and sisters, nephews. I have no one. He brought happiness to many other people. There are a lot of people mourning him." He swore viciously, helplessly. "It should have been me. I wouldn't have been missed."

He rose to pour himself another drink. She waited until he was settled beside her again. "Don't be mad at me, Joe. I'm just trying to help."

He shook his head. "No one and nothing can help."

"Yes. I can. You have to let go of it and go on. I'm here now, Joe, and you'll never be alone again. Never have to keep this all inside you where it will fester till it kills you, too. Life isn't always easy, always fair. You know that. Tragedies are a fact. People suffer them every day. I guess if there were no bad times, you'd never be able to recognize the good times."

Exasperated, he looked at her. "You sound like you're an expert on life, and look at you. You run through it doing goofy things and bouncing from one thing to the other."

Even though there was a tenderness in his voice, his attitude angered her. It was time for him to know. "You think you're the only one in this great, big, whole wide world who has ever been responsible for someone else's death? Well, think again. I killed two people."

He shot his cigarette into the ashtray and mashed it out. Putting his glass on the end table, he half turned in his seat to look at her. "Don't play games with me, Sterling. I don't like games."

"I had a husband and a son. Jerry and Timmy. Five years ago they were killed in a plane crash." She looked him straight in the eye, hoping she could find the courage to say all she had to say without crying. He put his hand on her shoulder and squeezed.

"Jerry was a pilot. We owned a Cessna 172. He and Timmy liked to fish at Manos Lake in Michigan. So they would fly up for the weekend occasionally and camp and fish and bond, as Jerry called it." She felt the smile that crept along her mouth at the memory of watching them together.

"That morning I drove them to the airport. The weather was excellent for flying. Timmy was jumping up and down with excitement and begging me to come with them. I don't like to fish, and I liked the idea of them spending time alone together, so I said no. I should have gone. Then I would be with them now."

Joe said nothing, just moved closer and pulled her to him, leaving his arm around her. A coldness gripped his heart. Her words were cutting to his very soul, twisting his gut, leaving him feeling helpless and grasping for something, anything.

Drawing a deep, steadying breath, she continued. "I was standing out on the tarmack watching Jerry go through his preflight when I suddenly had this chill and a flash of the plane going down. I moved toward Jerry to . . . to what I don't know—talk him out of it or just touch him to make sure I wasn't dreaming. Timmy climbed into the plane and pressed his excited little face against the window. He had his teddy bear under his arm. He was only four. He was waving to me and saying, 'Come on, Mommy, come on. I'll put the worm on for you.' I waved to him and promised him maybe next time."

She shook her head to clear the tears forcing their way to the surface. "Jerry finished his check and then he walked over to me, gave me a quick kiss, and ruffled my hair. They both waved and threw me kisses, and I let them go. I watched them taxi to the runway and then I turned my back for good luck so I didn't see the takeoff. God." A sob was torn from her throat as the memory tore through her. "Then I turned back and waved them off. I should have stopped them." She admonished herself with a sharp cry. "I should have asked them to wait just one weekend. A weekend! Or I should have climbed in with them. I should have done something. Anything." Her fists clenched at her sides. "Instead I did nothing. Nothing but stand and watch as my life took off in front of me."

Joe pressed her face against his neck as her breath shuddered from her. His shattered heart broke for her.

He was rattled. He was shaken to the very core. It plowed through him slowly. It all became so very crystal clear. This lady was barn-storming through life, driven by an unknown source, to keep from self-destructing. So much—everything—had cruelly been ripped from her that she literally squeezed every ounce of pleasure from every twenty-four-hour-period that she possibly could.

"Sterling, people have premonitions all the time and

they turn out to be nothing. You had no way of knowing anything would really happen to them.'' How quickly his perspective could change, he thought, as he watched her and wondered what words were suitable. Anything would sound shallow.

"Doesn't help. I keep conjuring up pictures of Timmy's face twisted in fear as the plane plunged toward the ground. I keep seeing Jerry's face as he tried to right the plane and I imagine his terror of killing his son. Did Timmy hang on to that damn teddy bear all the way down, or was he, please God, curled up asleep on the seat and never knew?'' Her voice wavered and he watched helplessly as she fought the overwhelming sadness. She couldn't prevent the tears now. Whenever she let her thoughts go this far, she couldn't stop the pain.

"I should have gone with them. That way we'd all be wherever it is they are. I want them back so bad. And I can't have them. Ever.'' She buried her face in his chest. He held her tightly and she could feel the tremble in his body.

"If you'd gone with them, you wouldn't be here with me now. I wouldn't like that.'' He remembered her reaction that day. So this is why the child in Delaware had upset her.

She held onto him for dear life. "Red wouldn't want you to suffer any more than Jerry would have wanted me to go with him. I know that. Maybe they're all up there together watching us. Hoping we make it. And by God, we will, Joe. We will.'' He saw the sparks fly from her eyes. She was angry now; determined.

"Life has become so precious to me. Yes, I probably come off as being a screwball to a lot of people, but I want to do everything, enjoy everything. Maybe that way, my husband and son can, too. I know if I had died, I wouldn't have wanted them to pull themselves into the grave with me. But I can't help feeling it was my fault they took off that day. If I had insisted, Jerry would have stayed on the ground." She was breathing heavily with emotion and exertion. Big fat tears glistened in her eyes, magnifying her resolution.

"Come here, kid," Joe murmured, and pulled her across his lap. "Rest your head on me. Don't think about it anymore."

"Hold me tight, Joe. I need you. More than you'll ever know. We need each other." She listened to the steady thump of his heartbeat.

He didn't say anything. Emotions were whirling roughly around in his heart. He'd been selfish. He'd never even considered that this bubbly, life-loving woman had known anguish. What she must have gone through, and all alone. Maybe one of his problems was that he only thought of himself. She was changing that. He kissed the top of her head and pulled her closer to him. He didn't want anything to ever hurt her again.

"Losing a child. Nothing, nothing could be worse. I can't even imagine the pain." He tightened his arms around her. His own tragedy seemed pale compared to hers. He had a bitter taste in his mouth.

She lay so quietly in his arms that he thought she had fallen asleep when her hand came up. She placed her fingers on his lips. He kissed them and she sighed and snuggled deeper into his arms. Pain merged with pain. Weariness joined weariness. But the simple closeness of their hearts and bodies began providing a slow, healing strength. He wouldn't sleep yet, but he hoped she would. Joe reached to light a cigarette.

ELEVEN

By the time he stretched to reach the ashtray and put out his cigarette, she was asleep. He listened to her relaxed breathing and smiled at the absence of perpetual motion.

It was funny how at night, when all was still, things seemed worse than they did in the daylight. Everything had seemed so much worse before this lady had come along. Was it possible that he could learn to live with this? Would other people let him live with it? He rubbed his hand over his eyes. He was tired. Tired all over.

Joe directed his gaze to the first, faint rays of light filtering through the windows. He didn't know. He didn't have the answers to anything and, frankly, he was very weary from the trying. He closed his eyes.

When he awakened, he was stretched full-length on the couch with a light coverlet over him. Sterling was nowhere in sight. Sitting on the edge of the couch, he rubbed his eyes and stretched. There was no sound of her in the cottage. Joe walked to the deck and looked out. There, on the very edge of the water, she sat, legs hugged to her and banded by her arms. Her chin rested on her knees.

She sat, staring out to sea, not moving. He recalled her words, remembered her pain. He slid the door open and walked out onto the deck.

The new morning sunshine glittered in her hair. The rays hovered over the calm ocean, glimmering like a jewel set in gold. He watched her a full five minutes. She would look out to sea and then turn her head back to study the waves at her toes. A gentle breeze lifted her hair and floated strands around her shoulders.

Somehow just looking at her eased his gut. He walked to the kitchen to prepare two cups of strong instant coffee. He set the cups on the counter and searched the cupboards for the jar. Plunking it down next to the phone, his gaze fell on the notepad.

The words jumped up at him and kicked him, hard. PROGRESS REPORT. NEWSPAPERS. NEXT WEEK. He picked it up and looked at the words a long while. He felt his anger rising. Other words swam in his mind to mingle with the ones on the pad. Betrayal. Hoodwinked. The fact that he felt his newfound trust dissolving told him he hadn't come to completely trust Sterling or his feelings for her.

So she was up to something after all. After everything, despite everything they shared in just a few short days, he'd been right. He had bared his soul to her last night, and she to him. It didn't compute. Like pieces of a puzzle shuffled like cards, his thoughts flew in all directions and refused to fit together as they should.

He tore the page from the pad, rage making his movements jerky. He charged down the steps and onto the sand. She heard him and turned to look at him with a warm smile of greeting. It disappeared as soon as she saw the way his brows were pulled together. He glared at her, eyes sparking fire. She shaded hers from the glare of the sun as she turned to face him.

He stood over her in his jeans, barefoot, bare-chested,

legs spread, and flapped a piece of paper at her. "Do you want to explain this?"

"What are you talking about? And who do you think you're talking to?" The freshness of the morning had begun to restore her, replenish her strength. She resented his destruction of it. And for what? Having grown accustomed to his unpredictability, Sterling stood up and brushed sand from her bottom. "Hold it still so I can see what it is." She snatched it from his hand.

"So?" She read the note and looked at him, turning her face from the glare of the sun.

"You're still going to play dumb, huh? Well, I'm not. Progress report—newspaper—next week? I was right all along. You're here to do a story."

How could he? How could he still doubt her after . . . But of course he was right, to a point. She fought to control her anger and be reasonable. "You . . ."

"Admit it! Damn it, just admit it. You were sent here. I was right. Talk to me," he demanded, stepping closer to her. His voice lowered and she could hear the threat in his words. "Was making love with me part of your plan or did you just start to feel sorry for me and decide . . ."

She swung at him but he caught her wrist, clamping his fingers tightly around her arm.

Wildfire sparked from her eyes and she bit her lip to keep from spitting words at him, words she couldn't retract later. She calmed herself by taking a long, deep breath and spoke deliberately and quietly. "Let go of my arm, right now."

Their eyes were locked on each other. Defiant, ominous, tempestuous. Both on guard and watchful, they stood a foot apart, one tall, dark, and menacing; the other small, fair, and daring.

He was the first to speak, keeping his hold on her arm. "Give me the answers I've been asking for."

"Let go of me," she demanded. She had already decided to tell him the truth, but not while he was like this. Not until she could calm the murderous inclination creeping around in her brain. He was so ready to condemn. So ready to accuse, so ready to forget everything that passed between them. He wanted it to be that way. Then he would be justified and his depression would be rationalized. It would be so easy to make all this her fault.

Sterling watched him, standing close, battling himself for his next move. He loosened his grip and she rubbed the circulation back into her wrist.

"It better be good," he shot at her and stepped back.

"No. Not now." She walked past him and headed for her deck. *Not now*, she thought. *Not when my heart is sinking, not when disbelief and confusion is all there is in me*. During the wee hours of the morning, he'd deserved the truth. Now he didn't. Not when he could throw the accusation in her face after they had helped each other through the night.

"Don't walk away from me, Sterling." His words were a taut warning.

She hesitated and stopped. In his voice, hidden in arrogance and accusations, was a hope that he was dead wrong. And he was wrong. Almost wrong. Mostly wrong. Even if she had deceived him for a good reason, with good intentions, it was still deception. She thought about the road to hell.

Squaring her shoulders, she changed direction and headed for his cottage. "The babies are hungry." She felt him close the gap between them and follow her up the steps. An old saying played in her head. One step forward, two steps back. He was practically growling as he followed her to the deck.

They both stopped short at the same time. Joe almost bumped into her. There, taped to the glass sliding door, was a picture. It was of Joe and his partner, Red. They were standing on an old porch, arms slung over each other's shoulders, big mischievous grins on their faces.

Seconds ticked by. Sterling looked from the photo to

Joe. His face was ashen, his mouth was open, and his stare bored holes in the door.

He reached up and pulled the picture from the glass, suspiciously, as if expecting it to disintegrate in his hand. "Did you do this, too?"

"Why you sorry son of a— Me? Why would I do a cruel thing like that? Why would you suspect me of being deranged when it's you who's crazy?"

He didn't hear her. He slid the door open and went into the house, directly to his closet. She followed him. Sterling watched as he dumped the contents of the box from his closet on the bed. Papers floated out and onto the floor. His police badge flopped solidly on the sheet. The little green crystal castle she'd longed for in the window of the shop rolled out to lay beside it.

It pinched her heart. He had gone back for it, but when? While she was in the jewelry shop, after the robbery, when she was with the old couple? Oh, God, what a sweet gesture. How could he be such a monster one minute and so caring another?

He was pushing things around and pulling things out and shoving them on the floor. Drawers. A suitcase. From under his bed, things were thrown around.

Sterling sat on the edge of the mattress and picked up the castle. He barely glanced at her as he searched the rest of the room and then headed for the living area to do the same. She held the castle toward the sunshine and watched the light fracture and dance.

Tears blurred her vision. Everything. All this blustering and accusing and anger was a cover. He had hung out his soul for her last night, but he still protected a certain amount of it. He had ventured outside the walls he had built for protection, he had swung on the gate a while . . . and now he was back behind the bricks holding the gate to be sure it was locked.

She heard him curse loudly and slam a cupboard door. Then nothing. Wiping her face and still holding the castle, she went into the kitchen. He was there, hands on his hips, shaking his head from side to side.

"What is it, Joe?" she asked, the toll the night and this morning had taken on her evident in the tiredness of her voice.

"My gun. It's gone." He let his breath out slowly.

"Your gun? And the picture. It was in the box, too?"

He turned to her. "There's something very wrong here."

"Besides you, you mean. Kids. Kids could have come in here. Nothing is locked up."

"No one has been around. No one. Not since I've been here."

"No one but me," she finished for him and maybe whoever was driving the car she had seen a couple of times.

He sat down on the couch and lit a cigarette, oblivious to her verbal digs.

She slipped the castle into her pocket and ran hot water for coffee. Dipping the spoon in the dark granules and ladling it into the cups, she fixed them a bracing brew. She heard the kittens stirring behind her in the box. They would have to wait.

She handed him a cup and he accepted it absently. She continued to stand in front of him and waited.

"I don't think you took the gun, Sterling." His voice was filled with defeat. "I don't think you did any of this. I don't think you stuck the picture on the door, nor did you call me and hang up or stash a copy of the newspaper with the coverage in it behind the couch."

His anger, his fear of what was getting started again, had controlled him. He hated himself, as usual. Mistakes, mistakes were all he could do . . . except for her. No matter what, this lady was the only good thing that had happened to him in years. She made him realize how lonely he had been. She made him realize all sorts of uncomfortable things about himself . . . and she loved him.

Walking to the door, she looked out, hoping the tranquil scene would ease here. "Your little gun is still by the bed. Why didn't they take that, too, if it was purely robbery. You didn't tell me about the phone call and the paper."

"I assumed they were just coincidences. The picture on the door was deliberate. The gun was stolen. Something is going on here that has nothing to do with you."

Determination gave her courage. "Since it concerns you, it has to do with me."

He looked up at her standing by the door. She was holding herself rigid, controlling her confusion and hurt. He loved her. There was no longer a sliver of a doubt. When he'd thought she'd betrayed him, only the fact that he loved her could explain the devastation he'd felt. And he'd barged out there and made a fool of himself. Again.

"Come sit beside me." It was time he took charge of his life again. She was right. Self-pity was ugly. Now that he could see it so clearly, himself . . .

"No," she spoke after a few seconds. "I have deceived you, Joe, but not like you think." She sipped her coffee and leaned on the doorjamb. Then she turned to look at him.

Cold fear drilled down his back. What was she saying? He couldn't have understood her.

When he started to come to her she held up her hand. "I was hired by someone to do a job." Her heart swelled when he wiped his hands over his eyes and leaned forward, his arms resting on his knees.

"His name is John Ramsburg. You wouldn't know him. Not many do. He's old, kind-hearted, and he's rich. Incredibly rich. When he hears about a tragedy, he tries to ease it. He sends me out into the field to secretly get to know the people involved. Victims of loss of all their property, children who are dying, old folks that are homeless or about to be. One of my clients was a little boy whose horse was struck by lightning as he watched. Mr.

Ramsburg put a yearling colt in his barn Christmas Eve. Elderly people on the verge of illness with monetary problems suddenly find this strange balance of money in their accounts. A dairy farmer was forced out of business by the government. So when his house went up for auction, I was there. I bid on it, purchased it, and returned the deed to his name. To this day he doesn't know how that happened. At least he can spend his remaining years in the only home he ever knew.'' Sterling paused and drew a deep breath. She couldn't read his reaction to her words.

''A hard-working truckdriver was on the verge of losing his truck just six months from paying it off. He had one child and another on the way. He received clear title. Mr. Ramsburg sends me ahead to validate the circumstances and inform him of the happiest solution. I make the decision. What do you think would work here, Joe?''

Joe's eyes narrowed.''You work for Santa Claus?'' What was she telling him? What was this crazy story?

She ignored him. ''He can't help everyone who needs it, but he does what he can. I've worked for him for five years, Joe. I've traveled all over the United States. He watches the newspapers and TV. He saw me on the TV news, at the funeral for my husband and son.''

Joe put his head in his hands and ran his fingers through his hair. She heard his heartfelt sigh.

She continued while she still could. ''A couple of years ago he had me watch a copy of that tape to explain to me why he chose me to do his field work. He said I was brave, strong, and proud in the way I handled myself with reporters and family all offering their hands to steady me, the sympathies to comfort me. I shook them all off. I made my way alone to a seat by the graveside services. If he only knew. I was dead inside. If I'd taken one hand or let myself hear one sympathetic phrase, I would have folded and never stood up again.'' She sipped the coffee that was growing cold.

Joe was leaning back against the couch now, watching her with misty eyes.

She had to look away in order to continue. "Ramsburg came to my house two months after the funeral. At first I thought he was a nut. But then he showed me articles on some of the cases and life stirred in me. I was needed. I wanted to be happy again. I wanted some place to dump all the love I had in me to give, somewhere else besides two shallow graves."

She took a long, steadying breath. "The will to live overrides the wish to be dead. I guess we should be grateful for it or the population would soon diminish as people mourned themselves to death. And you, Joe. He saw the news, read the articles, and he wanted to help you. So here I am."

She turned back and looked directly at him. "He didn't know I would fall in love with you."

He stayed on the couch and opened his arms to her. She had just given him all he would ever need. The words, the way she looked at him. This lady was all he would ever need again.

She moved slowly, set her cup on the end table, and then, kneeling in front of him, she went into his arms.

"I'm sorry," he whispered. "I'm sorry."

Sterling leaned her forehead against his. Reaching into her pocket, she wrapped her fingers around her castle and pulled it out. Opening her hand, she looked at the little piece of glass she held between them. "You knew how badly I wanted this. You went back and got it. What were you thinking about? Why did you do it, Joe?" She wanted him to think about why he dropped eighty dollars on a trinket for her. She wanted him to start exploring feelings that she hoped he had.

"I hadn't planned on giving it to you like this. I didn't know how or when, but I figured I'd know the right time." He put his fingers beneath her chin and brought her gaze back to him. "Can you forgive me? I've been crazy. Still am."

"Yes, if you can forgive my deception, good intentions and all."

"You said you love me?"

"I do." She smiled. "I was hoping you could tell." *Do you love me, Joe?* She asked the question silently. *Tell me you love me, too,* she pleaded.

Joe said nothing. He couldn't. Sometimes words came hard to him. He gathered her to him, his mouth raining soft, feathery kisses over her face.

Her mouth found his and she kissed him, gently at first and then wildly, passionately. He didn't need to think now, just feel. There was nothing left to hold back, no secrets, no reservations. He loved her. She couldn't feel this way about him, not to this extent, if he didn't. She knew it. But she had to hear him say the words.

His hands were all over her flesh, stroking, taking, demanding. Together they rolled to the floor.

Again, he was filled with patience, infuriating tenacity. He savored her, he reveled in her. More and more of him was lost to her every time their bodies touched. It was a good thing. A healing thing. A timeless renewal of emotion with every contact.

She was not patient, wanting him inside her, one with her, completing her. Her kisses became urgent, seeking. She pulled the snap on his jeans.

His hands ran slowly over the smooth skin of her breasts, her stomach, her back. She heard a moan of pleasure. Was it him or her? He was taking her far away, to a place only few lovers ever find. Across the ocean with the lightness of a sail, under the water with the heaviness of stone, through the sky with the skill of a pilot, he brought her senses to full alert. She thought she would burst into flames at any moment.

Still, he didn't stop, only slowed the languorous journey of his mouth over her body. Clothes scattered beside them, kittens softly mewing for attention, and the sun coming up strong, they took each other to new places—untried, unexplored, remote places.

When she thought she was drained, he showed her she wasn't. When she thought she would stop breathing, he gave her reason to draw air.

When he thought he had felt everything he could, she showed him he hadn't. When he heard nothing but the sound of his own heartbeat and his blood coursing through his veins, she whispered his name and he thought a man could die from loving a woman like this.

She positioned herself over him and slid slowly down. A complete union. Mind. Body. Soul. Again, they took each other through a dark, swirling, myriad of images and sensations. A coupling as old as time itself, new and exciting as if just discovered. And full of unspoken promises and love. Sterling arched her back and felt him grip her thighs. They were swept higher and higher to fall over the edge together.

Later, much later, she lay curled in his arms, resisting the temptation to sleep. "The babies are crying."

He laughed and rolled on top of her. "I don't hear anything except a few cats whining."

"You'd make a good father, Joe. Ever think about it? I've watched you with those kittens."

"You can keep kids in a box under the sink?"

She caught his mouth with hers and murmured against it, "Feed your babies, Joe."

The babies contented, fat and asleep, Joe joined Sterling on the deck. She was in a lawn chair with her feet propped up on the railing, as if they hadn't a problem in the world.

"We've got a real mystery here, Sterling. Who has my gun and why?"

She stirred and opened her eyes slowly. "The killer you two were after—they got him didn't they?"

"I assume they did. Everyone was there when Red died. I don't know. How could I be so stupid?"

"It's not called stupid, Joe. It's called out of it. You were a goner when I got here."

"IAD never said. All they were interested in were my movements, Red's position." He was astounded at his own ignorance and just how far he was from the life he had led. He had set himself adrift, hoping for destruction. He hated this.

"Ramsburg said something about reading the newspapers. I'll call him and see what he meant. Maybe he read something unusual. Could be the killer is dead. Maybe someone else is involved."

"It's dangerous for us to be here," he said, looking up and down the beach.

"If someone was going to hurt us, they've already had plenty of opportunity. Try to relax and we'll think this out. We're in this together, Joe. We'll make it through."

He ruffled her hair. "Always the Pollyanna, the Mary Poppins, except, of course, when I make you mad and you're Captain Hook making me walk the plank. I never thought I'd see the day a woman would be the most important thing in my life."

"Am I, Joe?" She pulled him to her. "Am I?"

A bullet cracked the air and hit the sand, spraying it, just off the bottom step of the deck. Instinctively, he threw her to the floor and covered her with his body. She felt the thudding of his heart and watched him try to peer around.

"What was that?" she asked, knowing the answer.

"Inside," he ordered, and shoved her ahead of him. He made a dash for his gun on the bedside table and was out the front door of the cottage in a flash.

Sterling crept to the window and looked out. Joe was standing in the open, legs braced apart, arms extended, gun in his hand. Every muscle in his body was taut and ready for action. His eyes scanned up the road and down.

He moved, changed his position, and carefully cataloged everything he saw.

She looked around, but saw nothing. No movement. No car speeding off down the road. No assassin lurking in the shadows. She took a deep breath and realized she hadn't been breathing for the last few minutes.

He came back inside. A determined line creased his forehead. His face was ashen. Fury pressed his lips together. His sharp eyes were dark and menacing. He paused to stand before her, absorbing her with his gaze. He had to protect her any way he could. "Nothing. This has gone too far. Pack your things and get back to New York or wherever you came from. Your Mr. Ramsburg's money can't fix this one."

He was gone from her again. In one split second everything was changed. Time spun backward and Joe Timothy MacDaniels was all cop. A wronged and dangerous cop.

"It still could be kids. Teenagers do plenty of dumb things when they're bored. You could have been spotted anywhere we've been. They could have decided to play with you." Even as she spoke the words she didn't believe them herself.

He snorted a laugh. "Just do what I said."

She watched him slide the gun down in his boot. He moved to his room and slipped his shirt on. "I'm going to take a ride around. Be gone when I get back."

He pulled her roughly to him and kissed her, a resounding kiss, and was out the door.

She stood for long moments after the sound of his Jeep had faded. Just like that. Be gone! Right. She listened to the sound of his disappearing Jeep. None of this made any sense at all. Joe didn't make any, either. Did he really expect her to pack up and run away from him and the situation?

To give her nerves time to settle, she took her time straightening up the cottage. She puttered around on the deck, watching over her shoulder and feeling uneasy.

Could he be right this time? Could someone be trying to kill him? Who? It was then she remembered Ramsburg's request. Read the newspapers, Sterling, just to keep up with the case. She checked her watch. Almost noon. Glancing around, she ran down the steps of his deck and up the steps of her own. She would call him and ask him what he knew.

TWELVE

Still nervous, Sterling fumbled as she dialed the phone. Forcing a deep breath, she tried again, this time punching the correct buttons. It rang three times before Mr. Ramsburg picked up.

"Mr. Ramsburg, how is everything?" She was determined to sound calm and serene. She would.

"Everything's shipshape here, my girl," he told her, clearing his throat.

"Good," she replied as she concentrated on his voice. It was good to connect with normalcy.

"How's your tan coming?" he asked absently, and Sterling pictured him going over a new file or scanning the newspaper.

My tan. Yes, my tan. That's important. "I'm a golden California surfer girl. Listen, Mr. Ramsburg, the last time we talked you said something about reading the newspapers. I haven't had time to pick up one. What was in there you wanted me to see?"

She noticed a change in his tone. "Why? Has there been some sort of trouble?"

"It's just been on my mind." She tapped her fingers on the countertop. There certainly had been.

"It seems that the deceased policeman's father has been making noises that the investigation wasn't complete enough. He, ah, he sort of believes that MacDaniels was negligent . . . and should be charged."

Was that all? She held up her hand, thumb up. Relieved, she remembered to ask, "The man who the police were chasing that night Joe shot Red. Did they get him?"

Ramsburg was silent a moment before answering, "You *are* getting to know MacDaniels, aren't you?"

"Of course. We just haven't spent much time discussing the incident. He's in pretty bad shape over it."

"Yes. Well, they did. He was pronounced dead at the scene. Pretty sorry character, that one. He'd been eluding the police for a good while. Spreading carnage along his way. I hate to think of it this way, Sterling, but even though the incident resulted in one policeman's death, in the long run it most certainly saved many, many lives."

Sterling heard her breath come out in a sigh. She hadn't realized how afraid she was to hear that the man might still be alive. "But Red's father is causing a fuss, huh?"

"Haven't seen anything recently, but right after you left, yes."

"Well, thanks for the information. I'll be in touch."

"Sterling . . ." he began, then continued after a moment's pause, "don't put yourself in any danger."

"Me? Danger?" That's a good one, she thought. "I'm out here lying in the sun and swimming as the weather permits. Joe and I are friends. I ought to know what he needs shortly. I'll call you. Bye."

She hung up the receiver before he could question her further. Leaning a hip against the counter, she tried to channel her thoughts, fought to put aside her growing feeling of dread. It could be just a simple thing. It could be. But she didn't think so.

Anxious, Sterling looked out the window for any sign of Joe. This is what it would be like if they did manage to make a life together. Always waiting. Always wondering. She shook her head. Other wives do it. She smiled, despite everything, and shook her head again. Other *women* do it. She wasn't about to tempt fate and actually start thinking toward the day they would be married. She wouldn't nurture that seed of hope that had evidently planted itself. Whatever kind of life they had together, it would be enough. But they would be together. She was certain of it.

Wanting to be busy, she took her castle to her nightstand and took a moment to admire it, touch it. Then changing to jeans and a T-shirt, Sterling walked out the front door and strolled down the road. She couldn't let her fears hinder her now. Too much had changed. Her priorities were different now. If she was going to face what she was afraid was happening to Joe, she had to do just that . . . meet it head on. Striving for casualness, Sterling held her head high and took the first step.

After fifteen minutes of strolling up and then down the road, she sauntered back toward Joe's cottage to wait. Proud that she had been able to take the walk without cringing, she approached the front door.

It was then that she saw it. She made her way carefully to the cottage.

Alerted now to the fact that someone could jump out at her at any moment, she looked back up the road and then down again. Straining her ears to pick up any unusual sound, she crouched down to inspect what leaned against the front door. Whoever was threatening Joe wasn't where he was looking. They were here, close by.

Leaning precariously against the door was a sizable piece of cardboard with the sinister words crayoned on it: "I could have had you anytime. Watch your back." Beneath it was propped a gun. Joe's gun.

Sterling looked around. She could almost feel eyes upon

her. Rebelling against this cruel trick, she bent and retrieved the gun and the cardboard. Holding the automatic in one hand, she pretended to look around bravely. Let whoever was watching see that she wasn't going to run and hide. Let them see that she wasn't going to scream and run away. They could have shot her or Joe at any time. They were playing a game. The cruelest kind. She silently prayed the gun was loaded and then added a P.S. that she didn't have to pull the trigger.

After a moment, she moved into the house casually, and then shut the door. Sucking in air, she leaned her back against the door and tried to slow the beating of her heart.

This was mean, twisted, demented. Who? Who would want to drive Joe over the edge of sanity? Red's father?

She hid the cardboard under the mattress and slid the gun under the pillow. She would give them to him only after she had time to think this out.

When he returned, Joe burst through the door. She was sitting in a chair by the sliding door, thumbing through one of his paperbacks trying to appear completely unruffled.

She looked up innocently.

He nailed her with a scowling look. "I remember telling you to get out of here."

"You did," she agreed. "I'm not going."

Joe paced. He stopped at the refrigerator long enough to pull a beer from within. Popping the top, he slugged the cold liquid. "You are."

She challenged him insolently. "You seriously think I'm going to leave you now?"

"You're leaving," he concluded.

"Be reasonable, Joe." She turned in the chair and propped a leg over the arm. "Two of us on the alert is much better than one."

He dropped onto the couch and lit a cigarette. "I can't watch my back and yours, too. You'll be helping me if you leave.' His words were forced through his set jaw and clenched teeth. His anger was very evident. He dragged a hand through his hair and tried not to dwell on her defiance.

"They killed the man you and Red were after. I called Mr. Ramsburg." She turned a page of the book.

Joe stared at her. Now nothing made sense. It would have helped if he had been right about that man coming after him.

He dragged himself up and walked to the doors. He looked to the ocean for diversion. Yesterday, hell, just this morning, everything looked good. He was really beginning to feel competent again. He had been given a glance at what life could be like and now it was threatened. He hated this.

"That information just makes it worse. That thug I can contend with. It's not knowing what or who I'm facing that makes the frustration factor very high." He sucked in smoke and expelled it furiously.

He was different somehow. She sensed it. He was holding himself straighter. His gaze shifted to see everything at once. His body was tense and ready to spring. He was all cop. Not the snarling, defensive man she had met when she first arrived. He was nowhere near the man who had taken himself out of life. The anger was there, but it was directed differently.

She liked the man she saw pacing around the cottage. Sterling understood this man. The one that snorted and walked back and forth and finally kicked a chair over to sit next to her in front of the door. She felt confident that no one could hurt them. No one could best this man in a fight. He was quicker, he was stronger, he was smarter.

"Not just what you're facing, Joe. What *we're* facing. What do we do now, Joe? How do we find out who is after you? You're the cop here. Tell me."

"We don't do anything. I know what I have to do. I expected you to be gone when I got back here."

"No you didn't." She grinned up at him.

He looked at her then, really looked for the first time since he'd gotten back.

She was stubborn. He'd known that. She was a Pollyanna and he'd known that, so why should he expect her to take this incident seriously? Because he told her to. "I'll drive you anywhere you want to go. I've got to get back to Washington and find out what's going on."

"You can do that from here. The phones work. Notify the police down here." She persisted. "It's their job to protect their citizens. And we are vacationing here, you know."

"Stop it, Sterling. It won't work anymore. You can't coerce me any longer and you certainly can't convince me that you're not the least bit scared of getting killed."

She slammed the book to the floor. "Oh, I'm scared all right. But I'm not leaving you. What do you suppose I would be doing back in New York? Walking in circles, biting my nails. Working on the reports for the next case, gazing off into the distance thinking about Joe. Wondering every time the phone rang what the news would be. Would it be you announcing you were getting on a plane to come get me." She paused only long enough to draw a deep breath. "Or there is always the possibility that you wouldn't get back with me at all. I don't plan on letting you go, not now. Not when you've become all that is right with me."

She went to the refrigerator and lifted out a Coke. Getting ice and filling a glass, she glanced over her shoulder. He was so still. If only she could read his mind. "Every time the phone rings I would wonder if it was the police telling me to come and say good-bye to you."

"That's what she said. My wife. She said she couldn't live with the uncertainty." His voice was a whisper. Sterling thought for a moment he was just thinking aloud.

He compared her with his ex-wife, who obviously hadn't loved him at all. That made her mad. She willed herself to cool down. "I'm not your ex-wife. I'm Sterling

Powell. I didn't say I couldn't live with it. I said, I'm staying here with you."

Dangerously calm, he replied flatly, "I won't ask you to."

She stopped with the drink halfway to her mouth. He wouldn't ask her to? She sipped the drink. "Ask me to what, stay or live with it?"

He turned then, his mouth drawn in a grim line. Tired, fatigue etched its way across his face. "Either."

Willing to let the subject drop for now, Sterling faced him squarely. "I see. Then there's certainly not much sense in continuing this altercation. How about a swim?"

He knew she hadn't completely lost her mind. He smiled indulgently. "Water's too cold. It's dangerous for us to be out in the open."

"Probably is," she agreed readily. "Dangerous and cold." She walked to the deck and sauntered brazenly down the steps. She should be explaining what she learned from talking to Ramsburg. She could tell him about what she found out front. She should be joining him in devising a plan.

Instead, she ran, fully clothed, into the ocean. The water was freezing. The shock of it had her moving quickly. Waves boxed her around and splashed her face with ice. She ducked under the first crest, hoping the even temperature would warm her a little.

She wanted to feel anything, anything other than the terror that wormed its way around her heart. She wanted to be cold, be miserable . . . anything but afraid.

She stood up, shivering, her lips turning blue. It was too early to even consider being in the water. Waving her arms to the man who was watching from the deck, she shouted, "Come on in, cop, the water's fine."

He shook his head. This lady was crazy. But no crazier than he was to care about her. "No way," he shouted down at her. "I don't get my boots wet."

She taunted him with names and teased and challenged

him until he walked down the steps to watch her. "You're turning blue. Get out of there. You'll get sick."

She didn't miss how his eyes scanned and took in everything, from their isolation on the beach to the way her wet clothes clung to her body. She was nuts. She had to agree with him this time. She was frigid. *Come out here, Joe,* she said to the waves beating around her. *Learn to let go. Learn to do all these stupid things and enjoy it. I thought you were beginning to understand.*

Cupping her hands around her mouth to assist the words to his ears, she shouted, "Some people swim in sub-zero-degree water every day. It gets the circulation moving. Makes the adrenaline rush. Come on. Try it." She challenged one more time.

He thought a minute and then stopped. He didn't like thinking. So far she had shown him that sometimes *no* thoughts were good. Action was better than meditation. He shed his boots, still not sure he should do this. He unzipped his jeans and shoved them down and off. The last to go was his shirt, and he threw it to the ground while he ran, lest he change his mind.

She watched, gleefully. He was a handsome man. His body was toned and tuned into a powerful machine of confidence and strength. She grinned at his nakedness. He was magnificent.

He ran to the water and, doubling up, cannon-balled into the first big wave that rolled in. The shock of it was enough to stop his breathing, but then it passed and he was cutting through the cold water, feeling very much alive . . . and very much in favor of drowning her.

They shivered. They swam. They choked. They turned a light blue. Their blood circulated to compensate and they wrestled and chased each other. For ten minutes, they forgot their problems and frolicked like kids on summer vacation.

Joe kept trying to put his finger on a brand-new emotion

that had stirred in him for her. It was still elusive. It niggled him.

He watched her. She was all things rolled into one. She was temptress, she was child; she was scatterbrained, she was deadly intelligent. He pulled her to him and tossed her back into the waves. Nothing could happen to her. And especially not because of him.

She was the first to break for the cottages at a dead run. He shouted and ran after her, scooping up his clothes along the way. By the time he reached the inside of his cottage, she had the warm water running in the shower and was half shed of her clothes.

He stopped in the doorway of the bathroom and watched unabashedly as she struggled to rid herself of her clinging, freezing-wet clothes.

"Help," she demanded between chattering teeth.

He walked over lazily and helped yank her T-shirt over her head. Her jeans were a little more difficult. They fought them together. And then they were in the shower, both reveling in the warm water. He reached behind her and slowly adjusted the knob until the water was hotter. They both sighed.

She threw her arms around his neck and leaned into him. The water plastered their hair to the top of their heads and rolled down cool bodies, to warm and soothe. She moaned, low in her throat.

He took the bar of soap and began to trace lazy circles across her back, down over her bottom and her legs and back up again.

She took the soap from him and lathered bubbles over his chest, his muscled arms, and his stomach and down . . .

The water beat over them. Steam filled the room. He lifted her and she wrapped her legs around him. Throwing her head back, she challenged him with a look and bit his bottom lip gently. He grinned and shifted.

He filled her. With one smooth motion, he was inside her. For a moment he held her still, hard against him. She felt him tighten within her. Sterling pulled him even closer with her legs. "My Joe," she whispered against his lips.

Later, the kittens fed and fussed over, Sterling sat on the kitchen floor with Elliott in her arms. "I think he's sick." She examined him. His eyes were shut again and he seemed to be so much thinner than the others.

Joe put the newspaper aside and watched them from his chair. He couldn't let her keep exposing herself to some unknown danger. He didn't fully understand why she kept insisting on it. Her head was tilted down as she talked soothingly to the kitten. She looked like a child at this moment. She glanced up at him and smiled. His heart constricted.

Clearing his throat, he sat back in the chair and rubbed the back of his neck with his hand. Aching tension made him touchy. "Nothing in this one about the case."

"Where did you go when you left here?" she asked him, petting the kitten.

"I drove up and down some of the streets. Not much action. A few cars. None I recognized. I picked up this paper and came back the long way. Nothing."

She had to tell him. She had put it off long enough. "I think it's Red's father. I called Mr. Ramsburg and he told me that he was making a fuss." She watched the expression on Joe's face go from confusion to hurt.

"Red's father. Sam?" he asked incredulously.

"He claims the investigation was incomplete. He thinks you were negligent and should be charged." She dragged out the last words, hoping to ease the cut they would have.

"Sam?" he said again, disbelievingly. He got up and began to prowl again.

She put Elliott back in his box and stood up. "Were you good friends with Red's family?"

"Sam lived with Red and his family ever since his wife died. Yes. I spent Christmas with them, Thanksgiving. Sometimes the whole family would go to the hunting cabin in Cumberland with us for a fishing trip. We went on picnics and I pushed the kids on the swing.'' The memories hurt, bringing new waves of pain.

She tried to picture that. This big, smoke-blowing, slightly wild-looking dragon pushing little kids on swings, gently, methodically, and probably smiling the whole time.

"Doesn't make sense then. Unless Red's father is losing it. Is he an old man?''

"Not that old.'' He made a move toward the phone.

"Don't, Joe.'' Giving him time to absorb some of this, she took his hand and led him to the couch. Pulling him down, they sat close together.

"I found something outside after you left. I have a feeling that if you called Red's house, you might find that his father isn't there.''

"What? What did you find?''

"Come on.'' She led him to the bedroom and brought the items out for him to see.

He read the message on the cardboard and handled his gun. He was glad to see it. The note . . . Red's father? He didn't think so.

He shook his head. "No. It doesn't fit.''

"Did you go to the funeral?''

"No, I didn't think it would make it any easier on the family. Besides, I don't think I could have handled seeing the kids just then. I went over a few days later, before I came here, and talked to Jessica.''

"His wife? How was she?''

"Just as you would expect. Shocked. Dazed. We were close. Brother-and-sister type thing. When she saw me she just held onto me for a few minutes.''

"And his father? He was there then?''

He shook his head in the affirmative. "He was just sitting in a chair by the window. He does that a lot. He likes to see what goes on outside.''

She knew he didn't want to suspect him, but she had to explore it. "Did you tell them you were coming here?"

"I don't remember. I think I told them I was going away for a while. I can't recall if I said where. Damn."

"I'll call their house and ask for him. What's the number?" She got up and went to the phone.

He was silent a moment, and then looked up at her. "Even if he's not there, it doesn't mean it's him."

She agreed with a shake of her head. "But if he *is* there, then we know it isn't."

He fished his wallet from his back pocket and pulled a crumpled piece of paper out of it, handing it to her.

She dialed the number and waited while it rang, afraid he would answer and afraid he wouldn't. No one answered.

Sterling returned the receiver to the cradle. "One thing for sure is that whoever is doing this isn't planning on killing you, just torturing you."

"Not necessarily so." He paced toward the door again and watched the ocean roll and pitch, ebb and flow. It hadn't changed. It hadn't stopped. It just moved on staunchly and refused to be bothered by anything. Eternity. The word floated across Joe's mind. He moved to stand quietly in front of the glass door.

"It don't mean nothin.' " He spoke the words aloud without realizing it.

Sterling heard them, and all her attention was centered on Joe. She got up from the couch to stand behind him. Putting her arms around him, she pressed a kiss to his back. "That is the coldest phrase I've ever heard."

"In the realm of things, all things being equal, nothin' don't mean nothin'," he repeated wearily.

Her voice was quiet and fierce. "You mean something, Joe. I mean something. We mean something. How can you say that?"

He continued to stare at the ocean, but he dropped his hands to his waist to cover hers; to hold tight to her hands. Tired, he explained. "Certain times, certain things. In

Vietnam many phrases were coined, but I guess that one got me and most of the other men through. Because when you think about it . . . nothin' don't mean nothin'. If you get blown up, you're gone. It's over. You're replaced by someone else. Anything that happened over there . . . it couldn't mean anything. If it did you could never have made it day after damn day. It takes a while to come to understand it. Maybe someday you will.'' He leaned back and just let himself feel how good it was to have her there. Behind him. Turning, he hugged her close.

"Teach me, Joe, teach me what it means.''

"I don't want you here,'' he murmured against her hair. He couldn't risk losing her. Not now.

"I go where I please and I please to be here with you, my friend.''

"You're not helping me. I need to know you're safe.''

"Sorry.'' She snuggled against his shirt and listened to the even beating of his heart.

"This person or persons might be planning on playing with me. Like a cat plays with a mouse until he weakens it, so he can kill it with one swipe. Just because our target died on the scene doesn't mean that someone else hasn't risen to take his place.''

"I can't picture you weak.''

He had to grin at that. She had made him weak. She had drawn the very life from him into her and then returned it ten times stronger. No woman had ever had the power over him that she had. In a way it threatened him. In another way it was a wonder to him. He ran his hand over her silken hair. He knew, right then, that his decision, made hastily when he had returned and found her still there, was the right one.

In the darkness of midnight, Joe walked barefoot around the bedroom, gathering a few things and throwing them into a small bag. His gun was tucked in his belt at his back. His boots were positioned by the door.

When he'd chosen what he wanted to take with him, he set the bag down and knelt by the bed. In the dim light cast from the other room, he studied her face as she slept, exhausted from making love with him. He saw the lashes that once raised would reveal eyes so stunning, so full of life that it scared him. He gazed at her mouth. Lips that had brought him such pleasure, and her hands . . . hands that held on to him so tightly that he felt like a louse sneaking out on her. But it was for her own good. Her safety. He had to find out what was going on, and he couldn't do it with her around. Not only did she split his attention, but she endangered them both with her unwillingness to face the seriousness of the situation they were in. One he had gotten her into. He could not live with hurting her. He had to go.

She stirred and he held his breath. He didn't want her to wake up. He didn't want to have to pull her hands away from him and jump in the Jeep and take off. He wanted to picture her like this. Wanted to remember the sound of her contented sigh as she fell asleep in his arms.

He stayed with her as long as he dared, and then crept toward the living room. Walking over to inspect the sleeping lumps of fur in the box under the sink, he shook his head. Yes, Elliott looked sick. She would care for them all.

When she awoke, she would be angry, but she would gather her things and go back to Mr. Ramsburg. Back to her safe existence. Even if she didn't, if she looked for him, she wouldn't find him. He hoped whoever was stalking him was doing a good job and would follow him out of there.

He opened the door slowly, and looking back for only a second, pulled it closed and latched it quietly. He hesitated only a fraction of a minute while the pain of leaving her tore at his heart. Then, engaging all his training and years of self-control, he jogged to his Jeep. Reaching in he put it in neutral. He pushed and coasted it away from the house. Jumping in, Joe jammed the keys in the ignition and twisted them, starting the motor. Stealing one last glance at the cottage, he pushed the pedal to the floor.

THIRTEEN

"How could he?" she shouted to the empty walls of the cottage. Furious and hurting, Sterling hurled herself around the house. She kicked one of his paperback books across the room. She set up the baby bottles, one at a time, slamming them on the counter.

"Just left you all here, too. He doesn't care about any of us. He just pretended to. He used us. We could have gotten a dog. A big one with long, sharp fangs." A tear rolled down her cheek and she swiped at it vehemently. She knew none of this was true, but it made her feel better to rant and rave. Otherwise, she would cry, and she refused to do that. She refused to shed a tear over that stubborn, obstinate, determined, pigheaded, opinionated, bull-headed mule. She was commode-kicking mad and she didn't care. She deserved to be. And then she had to smile. He was whole again. All cop. He was in control. She felt a surge of pride just before she felt the hurt again. She shouldn't be so hard on him.

One tear followed another. She licked at a salty drop.

She wouldn't cry, she wouldn't. Sterling gave up. Sitting on the floor next to the babies, she took Elliott out and hugged him to her and wept.

By the time she had the kittens tucked back in the box with full bellies, she had her plan all sketched out in her mind. She would go to Georgetown, to his apartment. She would find him. The first thing to do was to call Ramsburg and have her Porsche exchanged for a very dull and very large station wagon. She refused to drive anything around D.C. that would draw the attention of thieves. She was going to be too busy to have to worry about that.

Joe Timothy MacDaniels. He might think she would go away that easily, but he had a lot to learn about her. And she was going to see to it that he had the rest of his life to study her. She had lost one man and she wasn't about to stand by and watch this one slip away.

Sterling stuffed things in boxes, crammed suitcases and put them by the door. She had called Ramsburg and, without letting him get a word in edgewise, she had made arrangements for the other car to be brought out and exchanged.

Walking out onto the deck, she sat on the top step and stared at the ocean. She was going to miss it. But they could come back. She plotted. First on the list was to stop at a gas station and get a map. Flying into one of D.C.'s airports was definitely out. Airports were no place to be if you were in a hurry. Then she would have to arrange for a car, pick up her luggage, half of which she would have to leave here. And then there were the cats to consider. No, she had to drive. Besides, it would give her time to cool down and decide exactly what to do.

The gulls swooped and dipped to the water and then soared upward again. Their cries sounded lonely. She hadn't noticed that before. She hadn't stopped to realize how alone she had been before Joe. It would be that way no more.

Joe had left her to draw the stalker away from her. She

had to believe that. It couldn't be that when all his personality and character traits kicked in full speed that he decided he didn't want her. That he didn't love her. No, it couldn't be that. Being a good cop, he was going after whoever it was . . . not just sitting and waiting. It all made sense. She dropped her forehead to her knees. *I miss him. I want him to hold me.*

A happy young man brought her station wagon. She thanked him and took the keys in exchange for the Porsche keys and delighted in his exuberance to be on his way. She doubted he got much of a chance to drive a precision machine.

She packed the back of the station wagon with absolutely no thought to order. She slammed the tailgate shut with vengeance.

Gently pushing the box of kittens onto the passenger side of the front seat, she took one long look at the cottages and the ocean and slid onto the seat. If she took too much time remembering, looking at certain spots where they had shared special times, she would just delay herself. Squaring her shoulders, she popped the ignition switch and pushed the gas pedal. It felt like a Sherman tank climbing mud compared to the sleek black car. She shrugged. It was only temporary. So very much actually was.

The man at the gas station was very helpful. He drew a red line across the map and jotted down the road numbers for her to refer to on another slip of paper.

She folded the map and placed it on the seat between her and the kitten box. Fishing in her purse, she found her sunglasses and put them on. Turning the key in the ignition, Sterling sighed inwardly. She wasn't looking forward to this four-hour drive through unfamiliar places but it had to be done.

She pointed the station wagon north and rolled onto the highway and headed out. Any other time she might enjoy driving through towns with names like Salisbury and Kent

Island. She would be driving right by Annapolis, and had always wanted to see the naval academy. But not now. She punched the gas pedal and listened to the drag in the motor and prayed for no breakdowns.

Hours later, tired from the grueling traffic on 495, Sterling turned into another gas station for final directions. She had made a wrong turn for the last time. The kittens were howling for lunch, and she was thirsty and irritable. Dragging herself out of the car, she questioned the first man she saw. It turned out that she was only a couple of miles from the address she had for Joe. It was nearly two o'clock.

Georgetown was what she expected it to be. It teemed with life and had the flavor of years gone by. Derelicts littered doorways and Mercedes and Rollses lined the street. She had almost forgotten how nasty it was to be surrounded by asphalt and concrete with only an occasional scrawny tree straining for the sky and fresh air.

She drove around the block twice before she spotted a parking space, then cursed her decision to bring a station wagon. It was so difficult to park. She noticed that Joe's Jeep wasn't anywhere nearby. She hoped he left a house key outside somewhere.

After searching the top of the doorway and looking under the mat, she dumped the dead plant out of its pot and searched the dirt for the key. As a last resort, she turned the knob and found it unlocked. Unlocked! That was unheard of in the city. Unless, of course, you had nothing to steal.

And he *had* nothing to steal. The interior of his apartment looked much like the cottage at the ocean. No TV, a small, worthless stereo, lots of overflowing ashtrays, and a few empty bottles of beer. The furniture looked very old and worn. No pictures adorned the walls. The calendar on the wall hadn't been turned since April. A stack of *Smithsonian* magazines lay next to a few issues of *Playboy*. *U.S. News and World Report* was under a stack of unopened mail. She placed the box holding the kittens on the couch.

She walked to the kitchen. It wasn't as bad as it could have been. Some forks, microwave plates and glasses sat in the sink waiting to be washed. A can of automotive grease cleaner leaned against the bottle of dish detergent. A couple of car parts and a screwdriver adorned the counter. The phone answering machine blinked, indicating a message. The light was on for the automatic coffee maker. She flipped it off. The coffee appeared to be strong and thick.

Reaching the bedroom, she leaned on the doorjamb and smiled. It was the same. Dirty clothes, clean clothes. The bed was unmade. The quilt had slid down between the footboard and the mattress and forgotten. His bag, the one he must have brought back with him, was slung carelessly across a chair. Where was he? When would he come back?

She returned to the car and brought the bottles and formula in to get the kittens fed and settled down. While she fixed their lunch, she opened the refrigerator and looked for something to drink. Vodka was in the freezer beside plastic bags marked VENISON and SQUIRREL. A case of beer was on the refrigerator racks alongside two Coke cans. Not much else. Cheese. Olives. A jar of Miracle Whip. A container of jelly. Before she fed the kittens, she greedily drained the pop can.

An hour later, Sterling moved the kitten box to the floor and lay down on the couch. The drive had tired her. The waiting was exasperating. Her eyes drifted closed.

Horns blasting. People yelling. Tires squealing. Through the maze of exhausted sleep Sterling opened one eye. God, what noise. She had forgotten city sounds so quickly. She looked to the wall where his clock hung crookedly. Five o'clock. Rush hour. He could be at the police station going over clues. He could be in trouble somewhere. She went to the window and watched as life teemed along, ignorant of her worry and oblivious to her problems.

On impulse, Sterling turned to the kitchen drawers and searched till she found his phone book. Selecting the number of a cab company, she called for one. Going into the bathroom, she freshened up. She didn't overlook the faded aroma of his aftershave that lingered there.

Calling a cab was a mistake at this time of the day. Traffic was thick and snarled. She arrived at the 11th Precinct at precisely six, and she judged she could have walked it easier and faster. She paid the cabbie and pushed open the door to the old office building.

Shiny brass, dulled from neglect. Glass doorknobs and black-and-white tile floors. The smell of paper, leather, and humanity assailed her nose. The sound of voices; raised and muffled, typewriters and conversation floated to the ceiling. People sat everywhere on everything and anything. Some were handcuffed, some just slept. Uniformed officers and men in shirtsleeves sat behind desks or maneuvered their way around chairs and between people. Phones rang. Most were answered, but some shrilled on relentlessly.

Sterling spotted a young officer kicking at a vending machine. He smiled satisfactorily when a candy bar finally slammed down into the tray.

Making her way to the larger desk off to the right, she waited her turn to speak to the sergeant. "Excuse me," she finally butted in after waiting several long minutes. "I just need to know where I can find Lieutenant Joe MacDaniels."

"He doesn't work here anymore, lady." His answer was curt, and he promptly turned his attention to matters at hand.

She didn't give up so easily. "Have you seen him today?"

The sergeant looked up and examined her fully for the first time. "No. Who are you? A reporter?"

She thought fast. "An old friend from Indiana. I went to his apartment, but no one was there."

"He's on vacation somewhere," he stated flatly, and raised his hand in a motion to dismiss her.

Vacation. Uncivilized choice of words. Just as she opened her mouth to argue with him, she felt a timid hand on her arm. She turned to see a baby-faced cop about her own height smiling at her.

"I'm Tony. I heard you ask for Mac. You do know what happened, don't you?" His clear blue eyes were brimming with affection.

Relieved, Sterling put her hand on his shoulder. "I do. Tony, I've come a long way to see him. I'm Sterling Powell. We grew up together, Mac and me." She lied and used the rookie's name for him.

"Tony Bedford. He's quite a man, Mac. I really hated what happened to him and Red. There were no finer friends than those two. I was afraid it would kill Mac, too. I wish I knew where he was and if he's okay."

She wished she could tell him. His sincerity was touching. "Do you have any idea where he might be?" It was obvious to her now that he hadn't come back here.

"No. He just left after the investigation. Didn't talk to any of us. He just sort of faded away. I can give you his address, but I don't think he's there."

"No thanks. I have that. Is the investigation closed now? I mean, is Mac cleared of everything?"

Tony led Sterling to a corner desk and sat on the edge of it. "You know how things are around here. You hear things," he whispered.

She didn't, but she nodded anyway.

"They say that Red's father insisted that Mac be charged. IAD doesn't report to me, but sometimes I hear bits and pieces. I don't think the file is closed. Of course, that don't mean nothin' for sure. Could be the big guys are leaving it open until Red's old man gets tired of whining and faces up to things. Mac would've killed himself before he would'a killed Red.''

Lost as to what to do next, an idea struck her after a moment. ''Can you give me the address of Red's family? Maybe, just maybe, they've heard from him.''

Tony shook his head. ''I hardly think so, but I have it here somewhere.''

Sterling waited as the boy riffled through his desk. ''You never know. Mac may have wanted to talk to Red's dad or his wife.''

He copied an address onto another sheet of paper. ''Nope,'' he said with conviction. ''Mrs. Younger probably wouldn't let him in the house. They've all gotten kind of screwy since the accident. Shame. One man dies, but a lot of lives are changed forever.''

Sterling patted the rookie on the shoulder. His obvious hero worship of Mac wasn't dampened a bit by all of this. She admired him for that. ''Thanks for your help. If I find Mac, I'll have him give you a call and let you know he's all right. Okay, Tony?''

''Yes, ma'am.'' He grinned. ''I would like that. Mac and me, we were starting to be real pals. He was going to take me up to the cabin in Cumberland to hunt next time he and Red went up. I'd like to hear from him.''

Another idea struck her as she reached the door, so she turned back around to find Tony. ''Tony, how would you like to have three kittens?''

''Kittens, ma'am?'' he questioned, looking at her as if he had never seen her before.

''Someone dropped a box of kittens off outside Mac's apartment. You know him. He would drag them in and care for them, so I bought bottles and formula, but if I'm going to be traveling all over looking for him, I certainly can't take them with me. I'm sure he would be very grateful if you took them home with you. You could drive me to his place and bring them back with you.''

He thought a minute, and then his loyalty to Joe won

out. "I guess I could take them home. My sisters would probably love them, but I don't know if my mom . . ."

"Please, it's only temporary till I find Joe, ah . . . Mac. Then we'll come back and get them."

"All right." He said something to one of the other men and then escorted Sterling to his police car. It was a much better ride to the apartment than the cab would have been.

Once Tony and the kittens were on their way back to the precinct, Sterling decided to get to bed early and start for Red's house in the morning. According to the address, it was in Silver Spring, Maryland. Just over the district line. She was tired and had no inclination to drive to another strange place in the dark. Besides, Joe might come back here tonight and she would miss him.

She was hungry. She hadn't eaten anything except a very bad hamburger at a fast-food place on the way up. She searched Joe's cupboards and came up with some very stale crackers. She sliced the cheese and slapped some on the crackers, drank the other Coke, and collapsed on his bed.

She hugged his pillow to her. It was almost as if he were lying beside her. A dull ache began and spread throughout her entire body. She missed him. She wanted him with her for the rest of her life and, by God, she would see that it happened. She closed her eyes.

The next morning Sterling waited for the rush hour to be over. She went to Joe's closet. His uniforms hung there. Crisp, well-pressed blues. She ran her hands down them. His cap sat exactly in the middle of the shelf. What did he look like in them? All business and confident. She tried to picture him standing at attention with his hair cropped short, his sideburns trimmed. She smiled and brought one of the sleeves up against her chest. *Oh, God, don't let anything happen to this man. Please. Put a guardian angel on his shoulder*.

Red's house was the picture of modern suburbia. A two-car garage was attached to the rambling brick rancher. The yard was well kept and landscaped. A swing set was in the backyard. A big-wheel and a tricycle stood by the side door along with a ball and bat. An anchor fence enclosed it all, keeping everything safe and defined.

Sterling sat in the station wagon a long while. What would she say to these people? Chances were that Joe wouldn't come anywhere near this place, but where else? She had to start somewhere.

Knocking on the door, she could hear kids playing in a distant room. The door swung open and Sterling was faced with a huge man with flaming red hair. He wasn't smiling. His blue eyes surveyed her from head to toe and he just looked. He didn't say a word.

"I'm looking for Joe MacDaniels. Have you seen him?"

The man all but bellowed. She saw his chest heave when he drew a deep breath to keep from spouting words that would be rude. "No. Who are you?"

"I assure you I'm not a reporter or anything like that. I'm a friend of Joe's and I can't find him. I just thought he might've come here."

The man warred with his better judgment, but his politeness ruled and he swung the door wide to let her in instead of keeping her standing in the doorway.

The house smelled of apple pie. When she followed him to the kitchen she saw one cooling on the countertop. He pointed to a chair at the kitchen table and Sterling sat down.

The room was decorated with Pennsylvania Dutch hex signs. The curtains and the canisters were Willamsburg blue to match the toaster and the coffee pot. The table was covered with a crisp white cloth. In the middle was a fresh vaseful of mums. The place was spotless and smelled of Mr. Clean. Hallmark could have filmed a commercial here.

The voices of children became raised, and then two

redheaded boys streaked into the kitchen. One held a game board in his hands, the other the pieces.

"Grandpa, Grandpa. Jason won't play fair. It's my turn and he just keeps going and going."

The child was about seven, and as soon as he saw he had company he stopped talking and looked at her. The other child, around five years old, climbed up into his grandpa's lap and leaned his head back against Sam's shoulder.

"Joshua, whose turn is it?" The old man's voice was patient and gentle.

Joshua hid his little face in his grandpa's shirt and whispered, "Jason's," but then his eyes brightened and he continued animatedly, "but he always wins. If I don't give him a turn, then he can't win!"

Sterling hid a smile behind her hand. Joe was right. They were beautiful children. At least Red's wife still had them.

Grandpa cleared his throat. "Well, seems to me the object of playing a game is to take your chances. If you cheat you'll never know if you can win or not."

The little boy thought about this a minute. It still didn't suit him, but he decided to do as Grandpa said. "Okay. Let's go, Jason. We'll start over and . . ." Their voices faded down the hallway.

Sterling smiled. "Lovely children."

Grandpa was Sam again. "Shouldn't be fatherless."

Sterling felt the heaviness of his sorrow, only continuing because she had to. "No, they shouldn't be. I am sorry. But I know Joe. I know he would have done anything to prevent all this from happening."

"Coffee?" he asked absently as he got up to serve himself.

"Yes, please." She waited silently as he poured two cups and put them on the table. He set a spoon beside her cup and she added a good amount of sugar. Taking a sip, she was grateful for the warmth it brought her. Being in this man's presence had made her cold.

"Joe wouldn't come here. Not after the last time."

"What happened the last time?" she questioned, almost afraid to hear.

"Nothing. He got the idea he wasn't welcome." He sipped his coffee and eyed her icily over the rim.

Automatically on the defense, she tilted her chin. "It wasn't his fault. It was a tragic accident . . ."

"Did he send you here?"

"No." She laughed nervously. "No. I just have to find him. Do you have any idea where he could be?"

"Nope and don't care. Joe was always what I called a renegade cop. He used unorthodox methods to get the job done. Never anything completely outside the law, but dangerous nevertheless. He put my son's life on the line more than once."

"Cops put their own lives on the line every day, Sam. Not just Red and Joe. And they were narcs. That adds just that much more danger, increases the risk."

Sam studied her, appearing to make a judgment.

"I talked to Red about it. He always laughed me off. Didn't pay the least bit of attention to his old man. Now look where it got him." He chugged his coffee and got up to get more.

Sterling watched him. He was weary. He was tired. Probably the only thing that kept him going was the children in the other room. She could feel the sadness in this house.

"I can't tell you how sorry I am that your son is dead. But I must find Joe. Do you have any idea where he could be?"

He sat down heavily. "Little lady, if I knew where he was, I'd tell you because I don't give a damn. Last I heard he hightailed it out of here."

"Would Red's wife know? Maybe?" She realized immediately it was the wrong thing to say.

"Jessica hardly knows what time of day it is anymore. She comes and goes, sometimes hours, even days at a time. She spends a lot of time at the cemetery." He gazed out the window and Sterling could tell he was trying to keep control.

Still she asked, "But the children?"

"She knows they're okay with me here. I see to it they eat and get on the school bus on time and that they do their homework. Sometimes she's fine, other times she isn't." He returned his cold stare to her.

"Fixed that pie this morning. Just like nothing was wrong. Then the next minute she announced she was leaving for a few days and out the door she went. No telling. She has to work this out in her own way. It ain't up to me to say nothing."

"I wish there was something I could say or do, but I know . . ."

"There's nothing. I tell you it would'a helped if Red hadn't left that damn hunting cabin to Joe. The cabin, his shield, and his gun. When Jessica heard that at the reading of the will, she went off."

"The cabin in Cumberland?" Sterling felt an eerie chill work its way up her spine.

"Red loved Joe. Worshipped him. Wanted to be just like him. He had no way of knowing it would be some kind of a cruel trick on his family . . . leaving his prized possessions to the man who killed him."

Sterling stood up. "I think I'd better go. Thank you for talking to me."

The old man grunted and escorted her to the door. Sterling was glad to be outside, where she could breathe deeply of the air. She was beginning to have a really bad feeling about all this.

FOURTEEN

Her mind spinning, Sterling sat in the station wagon. Jessica comes and goes? She's gone for a few days right now? No. Sterling shook her head and put the key in the ignition. Pausing again, she sat back in the seat and pinched the bridge of her nose between her fingers. Could it be? Could Jessica be the one torturing Joe? No. She turned the key, powered the car, and headed back toward the apartment. This time she would search the place thoroughly. She'd go through his desk, his closet, look under the couch. There had to be a clue to where he went.

There was none. Pencils in need of sharpening, key chains, lighters empty but saved, a phone bill from 1984. A roll of Life Savers, soft and gooey, stuck to the bottom of the desk drawer.

Lottery tickets were mixed with insurance papers and old photographs. She lifted the lid on a little box and inside, haphazardly pitched, were medals. She picked them up one at a time and ran a finger over them. Pride filled her. He had done so much with his life. He had seen and tasted and spit out or absorbed more than she would ever know about. At least they would never run out of things to talk about.

She plunked herself down on the couch. Where would she go if she were Joe. Looking. But for what? Where would he start? She glanced around the room one more time. The flashing red light on the answering machine winked at her. She wasn't one for invading privacy. But the hell with it. She was desperate.

The first message was from a woman with a soft, teasing voice inviting him to call her when he got back. Sterling made a face at the machine. The second voice was Joe's. "Call 555-0090." That was it. Three faint beeps marked the end of the messages.

Sterling pushed the buttons and listened again. Call 555-0090. What did that mean? She picked up the phone and dialed the number. It rang four times and then someone picked it up. Sterling held her breath.

"Hello."

The rush of relief almost had Sterling crying. "Joe, where are you?" she breathed into the phone.

"Sterling? What the hell . . . Where did you get this number?"

"I'm at your apartment, Joe. You ought to be more careful. You left the door unlocked. Oh, Joe, I've been so worried . . ." Then remembering how angry she was at him for sneaking away, she cleared her throat and finished the sentence. "Where are you and why did you leave this number? What's going on?"

There was a pause and Sterling pictured him expelling his breath and looking at the ceiling trying to summon patience. She heard the decided click of his lighter and then the deep draw on the cigarette.

Sterling gave him a few seconds and then said sternly, "You might as well tell me. I'll find you. It'll just take me a little longer. I love you, Joe."

She heard him draw smoke again and blow it out along

with a few muttered curses. "I always leave a number in case someone is trying to find me."

"Someone is. Give me directions to the cabin, Joe."

"No. Wait for me there."

"Why are you at the cabin?" she asked, trying not to let the panic she was feeling come across in her voice.

"Look, Sterling. This has nothing to do with you. I have some things to find out."

"I resent that. You're in danger and it has everything to do with me."

"This is police business, Sterling. Stay out of it."

She gave up. "I have a bad feeling about Jessica. I—"

"Jessica," he interrupted. "Why?"

Sterling's hand fell on an old pack of cigarettes and she pulled a drawer open to find matches. "I went to see Sam yesterday."

"What? Why? I told you to stay clear of this."

She pinned the matchbook under her elbow to the counter and struck the match, holding it to the end of the slightly crooked cigarette she held between her lips. Breathing in, she drew to light the end and choked a little. Taking the cigarette between her fingers as she had seen Joe do, she answered, "Red said that Jessica had been out of town off and on and that she had just left again for a few days. He's been home taking care of the kids."

"So?" Joe asked impatiently.

"He said that Jessica has been acting weird." She took a puff of the cigarette and coughed, batting at the smoke surrounding her.

"Sterling, what are you doing?"

"Smoking."

He laughed at that. "Don't set my apartment on fire. Listen, relax. Jessica called and said she had some information for me. She said for me to wait at the cabin, that she was coming up. So, see, it's perfectly simple."

"Why didn't she come here? Why did she ask you to

go to the cabin? It *isn't* perfectly simple. You're a cop. You ought to smell a rat here.''

She heard him groan low in his throat before he spoke again. He pronounced each word precisely. ''If you and I are going to have a life together when this is all over, you have to learn to stay out of police business.''

Her heart tripped faster. She took a drag on the cigarette. It burned her throat and she blew the smoke out quickly and looked at the thing in her hand. ''When you left, you just told me to go home.''

''I'm coming to get you when this is all over. I don't want you exposed to whatever it is.''

That's what she wanted to hear. ''I love you, Joe.''

''Then do what I ask.'' He couldn't hide the fatigue in his voice.

Still, he didn't say the words she so longed, needed, to hear. And it was clear he wasn't going to direct her to the cabin. But she'd find it, regardless. ''I'll wait for you here. I'll keep the home fires burning.''

He laughed with obvious relief. ''Not literally, I hope. Sterling, you don't smoke.''

''No kidding. Joe, be careful. Don't trust Jessica. I think she's unbalanced.''

He was quiet a moment. Sterling put the nasty cigarette out in the sink. When he spoke, she could hear the love in his voice. ''I'll be home soon, kid.''

The line went dead at the click of the phone. She held the receiver to her ear a few seconds more as if to prolong her contact with him. She ached. She was scared. She wanted to be in his arms, lying on the beach with nothing to worry about except sunburn. Instead, she was standing in the middle of a teeming city, miles away from him, wondering, worrying what was going on. She pushed the button to release another connection and called Sam.

One of the children answered and then went off to find their grandpa, leaving the phone to klunk to the floor.

"Sam, this is Sterling Powell again. I'm sorry to bother you, but I need directions to the cabin in Cumberland."

"Why?" he bellowed.

"Joe's there."

"So?"

"I have to talk to him, Sam. Please."

The other end of the line was quiet.

"Jessica is going there, Sam. Think about it."

Sterling heard a weary groan and sounds indicating that the man had sat down. "How do you know?"

"I called up there. Joe answered. He said Jessica called him and asked him to meet her there. That she had some information for him. Sam, something is terribly wrong."

He was silent again. This time Sterling gave him all the time he needed to think. When he spoke again, his voice was strained.

"Yes. Okay. Take 495 to 270 to 70. About five miles this side of Cumberland you'll see a sign that says Twain Mountain Road. Follow that about five miles. You'll pass a little Mom and Pop grocery with gas pumps outside. Go exactly one mile from there and you'll probably see his vehicle parked on the side of the road. You have to walk from there. About a half-mile straight up. Road got washed away a couple of years ago. It's rough climbing."

Sterling scribbled his directions on an old, crumpled piece of paper.

"Thanks, Sam." She moved to hang up the phone when she heard his voice again.

She brought the receiver back to her ear in time to hear him say, "Be careful. Jessica isn't herself. She can't help it."

"Yeah. Thanks, Sam." So, he suspected something himself. Family loyalty.

Sterling ran to the station wagon to get her sturdiest shoes and her jeans. Changing in Joe's bedroom, she pulled open a drawer in his dresser and got out a T-shirt. Unfolding it and reading the front of it, she smiled. "Cops do it on the run" was printed on the front of it. She pulled it over her head and tucked it in her jeans. Yanking her hair back, she wrapped a rubber band around it and pulled it into a ponytail. She looked at herself in the mirror. She didn't appear terrified and panic-stricken. Good. After she sucked in a deep breath and took one more look around the apartment to be sure everything was turned off, she sprinted outside, slamming the door behind her.

Four hours later, glad to be out of the grueling traffic and on Route 70 north, Sterling played the entire scenario out in her head. It could be that Jessica hovered between sanity and insanity. After Jerry's and Timmy's funeral, she had been close herself, floating between reality and unconsciousness. And she'd wanted to blame anything. Anything other than herself. The fuel mixture had been off. But Jerry was a good pilot and she knew he checked those things. She'd accepted the explanation the officials had given her and had dismissed it. They had died because she didn't stop them. That thought nearly drove her crazy.

Jessica had lured Joe to the cabin, she was sure of it. She would hurt him. A woman was capable of hurting anyone that hurt her family. It didn't matter that Joe was almost part of that family. Times like this, it didn't make any difference. Jessica was scared—lost, angry, and desperate. The man she loved had been taken from her. Sterling felt sorry for her. But the thought of Joe alone with a crazy woman . . . She accelerated to seventy. She ought to see the Twain Mountain Road sign soon. And then what? She'd wing it, she said silently. Whatever it took, she was prepared to do it.

Sterling slowed the car and took the turn onto the narrow road. She clocked the odometer. The woods were thick on both sides of the macadam road.

On one side, the terrain—rocks and boulders—dipped away, dropping about sixty feet straight down only to build back up and away. The mountains were high here.

The sky was lost as she traveled farther down the road, trees arching and growing together forming a tunnel. Sunlight filtered through the leaves, glittering and sparkling reflections across the windshield. The other side went straight up. Large deposits of lime rock jutted here and there. Fallen trees rotted under a blanket of newly fallen leaves. She could smell the mildew, the moss, and the dampness. Rabbits, squirrels, and chipmunks darted back and forth in front of the car.

She imagined Joe and Red tramping through the forest, dressed in hunting camouflage, orange hats and rifles supported across their arms, pointing toward the ground. They would have small hunting licenses pinned to their backs. They would be chattering along the way. Camaraderie. Then later they would probably go back to the cabin, pop tops on beer cans, and kick back and laugh and tell lies about the day.

The Mom and Pop store came into view. It was an old cinderblock building painted white years ago. The roof was buckled, shingles curled. The gas pumps were ancient. An old pop cooler sat outside advertising Tru-Ade. The white had worn to expose aluminum and the orange lettering had faded to rust. A green dumpster sat by the side of the building, boxes and trash overflowing.

The road changed here. It became narrower and the macadam fell away to a gravel path. It was marked with pot holes, and more than once Sterling felt sure she had just knocked the front end out of alignment . . . along with her teeth.

There, finally, she saw it. Joe's Jeep. A warmth rushed through her, and her stomach floated. Behind it was parked the Chevy Cavalier. Bright blue and looking dead out of place in this setting. The dread set in, crawling through her and making her feel sick to her stomach. It weighed her down. What would she find when she finally made it to the top of the path?

That there was ever a road here was beyond Sterling's

imagination. Deep ruts cut down the mountain, and piles of rocks blocked her way. She walked and then climbed, tripped and scrambled, clambered and scaled her way up the incline. Catching her foot in a tree root, Sterling fell to one knee, bruising it and ripping a hole in her jeans. Not being prone to cursing, she surprised herself when she let a foul word fly.

She continued her ascent. Though the temperature was only in the seventies, Sterling felt perspiration dribble down her back and into her jeans. She brushed burning salt from her eyes and paused to catch her breath. She looked up. Nothing but more of what she had just been over. Scaling over a fallen tree, she shinnied up and over another pile of rocks.

The ground began to level out and the going became easier. When she was about to believe that Sam's half-mile must be five, she saw it. It was in a small clearing. Its simple beauty touched her. Sterling stopped, bent slightly, and braced herself with her hands on her knees and just took a moment to look.

The cabin appeared as if it had been carved from its surroundings by wind and erosion instead of the hand of man. Pine logs and white chinking, dulled and worn with the passing of time. And crooked. The porch dipped at one end. The roof bowed in the middle, and the tin curled a little at the edges. The windows were off square and in need of washing. It was early afternoon, and the sun played with the shadows it cast across the little cabin. She loved it. A time warp. And here she was in a century past. The stream that she had heard, but not seen, came into clear view. It traveled near the cabin and then dropped off into the ravine.

Should she march right up and open the door or should she creep around to the windows and peep in? She had no choice. The front door opened and two people walked out. Beside Joe stood a woman, a small woman with a head full of curly blond hair. They seemed to be talking

amicably about the weather. Joe had his hands stuck in
his pocket as he looked down at the pretty woman and
listened. He nodded and then seemed to look out and
around him. He spotted Sterling and, in his surprise,
shouted her name.

The woman jolted and disappeared into the cabin only
to come back a split second later with a gun in her hand.

Joe recognized the .357 Mag Colt Python immediately.
It was Red's gun. And she was pointing it at him.

Her tone of voice was one Joe had never heard before.
"What's that slut doing here?" she hissed dangerously.
"I saw you two on the beach, romping and kissing like
you were on some damn vacation . . . and all the while
my Red is rotting in the ground; where you put him. I
went down there to tell you I didn't blame you, and there
you were . . . with her . . . like nothing had happened. I
do blame you. I hate you, Joe. You're going to die like
my Red. You deserve it."

She emphasized her last words by poking the gun close
into Joe's back.

Joe's suspicions were confirmed. The muscles in his gut
contracted. He had begun to think he was wrong. He
wished to hell he had been. Jessica had been rational ever
since she'd arrived at the cabin. They had reminisced. It
seemed to help her to talk about Red and he had let her.
He had noticed a blankness that would come over her now
and again. He had also noticed that in the three hours she
had been with him, she hadn't once looked him in the
eye.

When Jessica had called him and requested that she
meet him at the cabin and had declined his offer to simply
come to her house and talk, the pieces had begun to fall
together. This lady wasn't handling things too well, that
maybe, just maybe, she had gone off the deep end. Suspecting a real hood of doing any of the things at the beach
just didn't fit. If one of them wanted to off him, they
would simply have done it.

Joe held his hands up in the air. "Jessica, put the gun down. You might · just blow a big hole in me. Put it down."

"No. You don't give the orders anymore. I want you to suffer. I want you to die. Why should you be alive and my Red dead? It should have been you." Her eyes were wild and her lips curled back with every word. The dangerous hissing sound was replaced by a voice not at all like her own.

Sterling wasn't breathing. She forced herself to take one small step at a time while keeping her eyes glued to the woman with the gun. One wrong move and it would all be over. Just a little bit too much pressure on the trigger and her Joe and her whole life would go away right in front of her eyes. Again.

If she could get Jessica's attention away from Joe, if she could get her to point the gun at her, Joe could grab it away from her and maybe . . .

Sterling could hear the blood pounding through her head. She heard Joe talking to Jessica. Heard his even tone and wondered how he could sound so calm. Sterling felt as if she were being held under water. She couldn't breathe, couldn't see clearly.

Jessica began again, in a singsong voice that floated eerily on the fresh, clean mountain air. Sterling realized how isolated and alone they were here. That woman could kill both of them and they might not be found for years. Sterling moved closer to the cabin. She saw Joe flash her a look that meant for her to stop. She did.

Birds flew overhead, singing and chirping greetings to one another. Something, to her right, bounded through the trees and the undergrowth. God, how could this be happening?

Jessica's hands shook slightly as they supported the gun. Joe moved slowly and easily to lean back against the railing. He kept his hands where she could see them.

Mustering his commanding voice to full tilt, he said,

"I know how you feel, but killing me . . . that would only take you away from your kids. They need you."

"Never find you up here." She laughed. "Not until you're a skeleton. I don't care anyway. Red is dead. You should be dead." She began to shake and then, as if suddenly remembering Sterling, she directed the next sentence to her without taking her eyes off Joe. "Get up here, girlie. Stand next to your boyfriend here and maybe some of his blood will splash on you as he goes down."

Sterling found her voice. "I'm coming. Jessica, I stopped by and saw your kids before I came up. They were playing a board game and Joshua was winning." Normalcy. Maybe that's what she needed. It was sure what Sterling needed. Craved.

She saw Jessica waver, as if part of her brain was trying to get through to her, and then a steeliness crept into her eyes. "Get on up here. Stand by your man." That made Jessica laugh even harder, a high-pitched, frenzied sound that hurt Sterling's ears.

Joe made a move forward and Jessica steadied the gun, aiming right between his eyes. "No. Don't move. I'm not going to kill you right now. Don't make me. I want you to be scared. I want you to suffer. I want you to beg me. Did Red beg you to help him?"

A stab of guilt pierced Joe's heart. Maybe it was divine justice. Maybe he would end up an unidentified corpse in the woods, but now Sterling was here. He couldn't let anything happen to her. He could take a chance . . . make a swing for the weapon. He could jump Jessica. Chances were he could make the move before she squeezed off a shot. But he wasn't taking any chances. Not just yet.

Sterling walked up the steps slowly. They creaked and gave under her slight weight. "You have a beautiful house. The kitchen is decorated very nicely." That her voice sounded almost normal surprised her. She forced herself to continue. "The boys are handsome, too. And that apple pie you baked this morning. It smelled good."

Jessica seemed to calm, but her grip on the gun remained. She didn't take her eyes off Joe. "I make good pies. Crust is flaky. Red likes it that way. He's a big man and needs lots of food. Later, we'll have some after the kids go to bed and Sam is settled in his room. Later . . ." She began to wail, a shrieking, mourning sound. "There's no later. He's not coming home."

Sterling looked at Joe. There was pain in his eyes, not fear. He was sick. He was blaming himself for the loss of another human being. The one standing so unsteadily, yet strongly, in front of him. She had been almost sane until she saw Sterling. Maybe he could let her calm down, talk her out of it.

Sterling reached Joe and flung both arms around his waist. He wrapped an arm around her shoulder and squeezed. Now that Sterling was holding Joe, the reality of the trouble they were in finally struck her. She trembled as she looked down the barrel of the gun.

"Isn't that cute," the deranged woman leered at them. "Yeah, I saw you on the beach. I spied on you through the window. You two were so wrapped up in each other you didn't even see me. I was quiet." Her voice changed to a whimper. "It isn't fair. You can make love and I can't."

She's going to pull the trigger without even meaning to. The thought struck Sterling to her very core. Jessica would pop off a round and it would all be over and she'd be sorry and put away. No. It couldn't happen.

Sterling looked directly at Jessica instead of the gun. Pushing her all-consuming fear aside, she straightened. "Jessica. Joshua, how old is he now?"

Jessica was silent. She was straining to keep the gun up and pointed at Joe. She opened her mouth, but no words came out. Sterling could tell the wheels of memory were turning, trying to get through the blockage. "Seven. He likes school."

Steeling herself against her own words, Sterling began.

"My little boy, Timmy, would have been nine this year. I lost him, Jessica. I lost him in a plane crash along with his daddy."

Jessica's eyes went to Sterling and so did the point of the gun. Sterling pulled in her breath and waited. She watched as Jessica warred with her thoughts. "So what. You want me to feel sorry. You want *me* to be sorry?"

"I want you to realize that you can go on without the people you love. Red can never be replaced, but you can be happy again. Red would want that for you. He loved you. And those two little boys love you."

The whining began again, and for a moment Sterling thought the bullet was coming. "They do. He did. He was good to me. He was good to everybody."

Joe spoke up authoritatively. "Then put the gun down. Let's talk."

Jessica giggled. "No way. Go in the house. Both of you. And don't come too close to me or I'll do it now. I'll give you some time together before I kill you, Joe. A little bit of time. Just enough to make you wish I would get it over with. Now, move."

Jessica stepped to the side, following Joe with the gun as they moved into the house.

FIFTEEN

The inside of the cabin was dim but Sterling could make out the braided rugs and heavy pine furniture. The floor that was once bright had dulled. Deer heads were mounted on the walls. Rifles hung over the fireplace. Empty, no doubt. A round table sat in the kitchen area. After demanding that Joe and Sterling take a seat on the couch, Jessica sat on a chair behind the table and laid the gun down . . . making sure she kept a finger on the trigger and the barrel pointed at them. She glowered at Joe with bloodshot eyes.

Sterling rested her head on Joe's shoulder. She heard him whisper, "I love you."

Tears wanted to fall. She yearned to jump up and scream. She ached to throw something at her. Anything. This all had to stop before it went too far. And now he says he loves her. It should be the happiest time, the best of times. He said the words. At the point of a gun. Her temples throbbed.

Beside her, Joe's body was rigid. His muscles were

206

tense. Sterling sensed that the wheels in his brain were turning furiously.

A lousy mistake, one damn lousy mistake and this woman could be shooting. Shooting him. Shooting Sterling. He knew that she couldn't possibly realize the power of the weapon she held so tenuously under her hand. He knew she didn't realize that once she squeezed the trigger, she couldn't call back the bullet. She couldn't simply say whoops and I'm sorry. And now Sterling was here. Despite all his efforts to keep her clear of this mess, she was right in the middle of it. It made it harder for him. He could have taken his chances making a dive for the gun at some point, but now . . . now she could be in the line of fire. If and when they got out of this ordeal, he was going to be sure she understood the word "no."

He felt for her hand and took her slim fingers with his square ones. Squeezing, she held on for dear life.

Down at the bottom of the path to the cabin, Sam looked up at what he had to scale. He must be as crazy as the rest of this bunch, he thought to himself. Hitching his trousers higher around his waist and tightening his belt, he began the climb. Praying he was wrong.

Jessica was tiring. Joe could see it. His dry sense of humor made its way over everything else. It must be very draining to be crazy. Now what? They could sit here and be at the mercy of this poor sick woman? He didn't think so.

Engaging his priestly tone of voice, Joe spoke in quiet, even tones. "You're tired, Jessica. Why don't you forget all this and I'll drive you home. Your children need you. Sam needs you."

"I am tired, Joe. Sometimes so tired I can't get out of bed."

Sterling wondered why it seemed that right now, at this very moment, they were all having a Sunday morning conversation over coffee and doughnuts. She wriggled in her seat, and Joe tightened his grip on her hand to warn her not to move too much.

Suddenly, Jessica jumped up from the table, taking the gun with her as if filled with new energy. "Remember the time we were all up here and got snowed in. God, that was a week. You two ran out of beer after the first three days. You flipped a coin to see who was going to hike down to the store and carry a case back. You lost, Joe, and Lord did you look silly with icicles hanging off your ears and two cases of beer on that damn American Flyer."

Joe pretended to be relaxed. He slung his arm across the back of the sofa and laughed. "Well, why go down for one when you can haul two.

Jessica moved to stand in front of the window and leaned back against the sill. "Yeah, but we didn't even have rolls for the hot dogs. You forgot those. So we ate them plain, dipped in ketchup, like french fries."

If he could get her mind flowing with memories, maybe he could wander over close and simply lift the gun from her hand. "And we went out and built the snow animals. What was it? A big rabbit and a bear, I think."

She shook her head, laughing but never lowering the gun beyond her waist. "And then the snow forts went up and we had a snowball battle to beat all. We were frozen and hungry when we finished that up. God, what a time we had."

"Good thing the kids weren't with us that time. It would have been hard to keep them occupied. It was hard enough for us to find things to do." Joe moved, only a little, away from Sterling, and dropped her hand.

"Played poker till we had nothing left to lose. And then you two began making up songs on that old guitar." She dragged one hand through her hair, the gun weighing down the other.

Sterling felt Joe begin to get up. He made it to a standing position before Jessica looked directly at him again. She seemed to have forgotten why they were all there.

She looked up at him, eyes shining with the good feeling the memories brought her.

Joe lit a cigarette, drawing deeply, and wished desperately for a drink. He carefully and slowly moved to the stereo and punched the button. The room was filled with country music. Willie Nelson was punishing himself with "You Were Always on My Mind."

Sterling watched as Jessica followed him with her eyes. And the gun. Joe was talking. A light tone, one of fond remembrance. Jessica answered him with a pretty smile. He made his way cautiously across the room. "How about the time we took the kids to the lake and we all fell in when you stood up in the rowboat?"

She laughed hard then, not paying any attention to the gun. As Joe closed the gap between them, she skidded near the edge again. Her head flew up and her eyes sparked with fire. She put both hands around the gun and fired it at the floor exactly between where Joe stood and Sterling sat on the couch. The shot echoed around the room and deafened Sterling. Joe froze. Wood split and splinters flew. He didn't look at the floor. He knew what the hole would look like.

"No, no, no!" she shrieked. "Sit back down, Joe. Or the next hole is in you. Don't you want some time to say good-bye to that cupie doll over there?"

"As a matter of fact, I would." Joe walked over and sat down, trying to keep his eyes off the hole ripped in the floor. He directed his attention to Sterling. Jessica had to sleep sometime, he decided. He would have to wait until then.

He looked at his precious Sterling. She had brought him alive again and might just be around to watch him die once more. It was her own fault. If she'd just gone home like he told her to. There was fear in her eyes along with something that could only be described as an energy of protection when someone you loved was in danger. He prayed she didn't make a stupid move.

Jessica was up and pacing again. She was making sounds, not forming words. Sterling braced herself for the moment she would discharge the gun again and tucked a possessive hand through Joe's arm.

Sam heard the shot and stopped. He was puffing. He wasn't as young as he used to be and this damn path just kept getting worse. *I'm too late*, he thought. He had followed them up here as fast as he could. He should have seen it coming. He had. But he'd ignored it. He thought it would go away. After all, grief was a terrible thing. It made people act strangely. There was no real reason why he should have believed Jessica would actually hurt someone.

He made it to the clearing and looked up at the cabin. Sam could see her there, through the window, walking back and forth with the weapon clenched in her hands. He swiped a tired hand across his forehead. And he had thought things couldn't get any worse. He trudged up the steps and swung the door open wide.

It was all the diversion Joe needed. Jessica swung around when Sam opened the door. The big man stood there, taking in the scenario in one swift glance. He called out to Jessica.

With the sun shining in from behind him, glinting off his mane of red hair, Jessica thought she saw her husband. "Red!" she cried and went to move toward him, gun swinging from one hand at her side.

Seconds ticked by. Heavy seconds. Joe let her get positioned with her back to him and then Joe lunged, grabbed, and dove to the floor, the gun caught safely in his hands; between himself and the braided rug. He sighed audibly, and let his forehead rest on the floor. He had the automatic. Everyone was safe.

Jessica let out a feral, blood-curdling scream and collapsed in Sam's arms. Sam gathered her close and held her, tears streaming down his face, his sad eyes on Joe.

Sterling threw herself down beside Joe. Her bruised

knee objected, but she ignored it as she buried her face against his back. She heard his heart tripping quickly and felt his second sigh of relief.

"Are you okay?" he asked, turning his head just enough to look at her.

"Yes." She didn't know. "Are you?" Sitting back on her heels, Sterling wiped her hands over her eyes.

"Yep."

"Then why are you lying on the floor with the gun under you?" A nervous, wary smile played across her face.

"I wanna beer," he stated dully.

She sat back flat on the floor and braced herself with her hands behind her. "And a chaser." What *she* wanted was a bottle.

Sam had moved outside with Jessica. They could hear her sobbing, hear the creak of the porch swing as he rocked her. Jessica made a weak and draining sound. Maybe now she could start rebuilding her life instead of trying to destroy it.

Joe rolled over and lay flat on his back and studied the ceiling. Not once did he really admit that he thought this would end with someone getting killed. Not once did he let on that his stomach was churning, that his palms were sweating or that his mind was reeling from trying to figure a way out of this without hurting Jessica.

"I'll call Mr. Ramsburg. He'll see to it that she gets the help she needs," Sterling offered.

"Good idea," Joe agreed. He wanted that drink, but he was too strung out to move.

Sterling pushed the lethal weapon away from both of them with her finger. "A couple of times there I was really afraid we weren't going to make it."

"Not me." He lied so well. "I believe in fairy tales now, you know. I've had a good teacher." He turned his head to look at the woman he loved. "Someone who wouldn't give up when I told her to. Someone who didn't

quit when I seemed a lost cause. *You*, Sterling. Somewhere along the line, *you* did it. You made me think. You
forced me to feel all the things I had stored away. I don't
think I'll ever forgive you for it," he teased. He was
going to do a lot of that in their lifetime.

She punched him and then stretched out full length
beside him, pressed a kiss to his shoulder, and rested her
hand on his rib cage. "Even the part about living happily
ever after?"

He groaned and grinned at the beamed ceiling. "Especially that part. You endangered all of us, you know. If
you had only done what I told you and waited."

She got up and went to the refrigerator. She pulled two
beers and popped the top on one and drank from it greedily. She took the other one to him and stood over him
with it. Popping the top of that one, she began to tip it,
threatening to drench him with it.

Joe shot up. Taking the beer, he sipped and headed
back to the kitchen to find the bottle of Jim Beam. After
opening several cupboards, he found the half-full bottle
and a shot glass. He tipped the glass and emptied it, then
poured himself another.

Sterling came to stand with him. Her nerves were making her act so giddy. If she stopped and took the time to
think, she would be a weeping mess and she'd have none
of that. She braced herself against the kitchen counter and
waited for the weakness to leave her limbs. She noticed
the sounds on the porch had ceased.

Sam came to the doorway. He was pale and his eyes
were red. His daughter-in-law was still propped up by his
huge arms. Jessica looked dazed and lost; she didn't even
look up at them.

"I'm going to take her to a hospital."

Joe turned and leaned a hip on the counter. "You want
some help?" He hoped he didn't. He didn't feel like
climbing down the mountain. He wasn't the least bit

inclined to continue his association with Red's family at this moment.

Sam shook his head. "No, but thanks." He turned his direct gaze on Joe. "I'm sorry."

Joe dismissed that with a wave of his hand. "Just take care of her."

Sam and Jessica disappeared.

By now the sun was low in the sky. A breeze had picked up and Sterling could hear the stream rolling along, bubbling over the rocks and dropping down the ravine. It was the first she had heard it since she entered the cabin. She let the sounds settle her.

They both stood there, drinks in their hands. The shock, the daze, the full effect of what had happened began to wear off.

"Let's go sit on the swing." Without waiting for an answer, Joe took her hand and led her outside. It was getting chilly. Joe pulled her close to him and put his arm around her. With one foot pushing against the floorboards, Joe put the swing in motion.

"I heard you say you love me."

"I was under a lot of pressure." He did love her, but he didn't quite know how to handle it yet. He still needed time to digest everything. Besides, the knowledge made her almost smug. A warmth spread throughout his body as if his circulation had just kicked back in. The reality. The cold reality was that he almost lost her. Lost her and what they could have together. The thought made him shiver.

She felt it move through him. "Do you want a flannel shirt? I saw one tossed across the chair." If he didn't, she did.

"Don't move just now. Just be still. Just be here with me."

She snuggled closer. His body was warm. If this had turned out any other way . . .

"I'm pretty upset with your coming up here after I told

you to stay put." It had to be said. She had to realize that she couldn't continue to go through life doing any damned thing she pleased.

Sterling thought he was teasing at first, but when he didn't laugh she turned her face to study his. "You told me to stay put. I thought you suggested it. I don't like to be told what to do."

"I figured that out. You really threw this all off. I was handling things just fine until you showed up and panicked her."

"Are you trying to tell me that you had this all figured out? That you knew it was Jessica that was doing these things? That's bull and you know it." She pushed away from him so she could be sure she didn't miss anything his eyes could tell her.

"Of course I knew. I'm the cop, remember. I started suspecting as soon as I saw the picture on the door. A street thug wouldn't be so delicate. When she called and insisted that I meet her up here, I was pretty sure."

"Why didn't you tell me?" She practiced her patience.

"Where are the kittens?"

"Joe. Why didn't you tell me?"

"For precisely the reason you think. I knew you would come up here and screw up everything."

The anger canceled out her concern. "Oh, you did, did you? Did you ever consider the fact that if you'd told me I might have been content staying in Georgetown knowing you could handle the situation?"

"No. I've never seen you deny yourself anything so far."

"That's cold, Joe, and unnecessary."

"It's vital." It was. If she was going to be his wife she had to understand that police business was just that. Business, not something for her to dabble in just because he did.

She realized he was tired, strained. But he would have

to learn to accept her for who she was. She would never be easy to control.

Returning his gaze to her, he took her hand. "I'm going back."

Elated, Sterling planted a kiss on his stubbled cheek. "The beach. Great. But I think it's beautiful here, too. Could we stay here a couple of days first?"

"I'm going back to the force." He held tight to her hand and tried to gauge her reaction. Something flitted across her eyes and then disappeared. Her fingers tightened on his.

Mentally and physically exhausted, she fought tears of lassitude and alleviation. "Stop the swing, Joe. When did you decide this?"

"I don't know. Sometime in the last twenty-four hours. I'm needed. I have a job to do. It's me, Sterling. It's what I do best." Though he was tired, his eyes were clear. Clearer than she had ever seen them. He was better. He was alive again.

Yes, she knew it was him. Standing up, Sterling went to the railing and looked out around her. Had she come to hope he would give it up as he had said he would? Had she come to wish for a normal life of safe days and secure nights? Maybe part of her had, but the other part knew. She had wanted it to last a little longer. That's all. Just a little longer.

"And if you're going to be my wife, Sterling, you have to learn to go about your fairy-godmother chores and leave the police business to me."

His wife? His wife! He hadn't even said he loved her and he was proposing. Or was he issuing orders? Was he plunking things down in front of her to see how she set them in order?

Joe hated that he wasn't better with words, better at saying exactly what he felt. He waited for her to move, to give him some hope that she wasn't going to simply break his arm and march back down the path to her little wonderland existence. He stood up and pressed himself against her, circling her with his arms and pulling her back to rest against his chest.

"Joe, all along I've been fighting to get you back to where you are now. Do you think it was simply for you or just for Mr. Ramsburg? At the beginning it was. Then somewhere along the line I fell in love with you, J.T. MacDaniels. It's not whether I can handle your being a cop. The question is, can you handle my being your wife? I'm not docile. I won't simply sit around and knit. And if ever, ever you are in danger and I know about it, I will be there."

Relief flooded through him, and then the love between them soothed and eased him. He felt invincible and he liked it. He had her to thank for that. And so much more. "Was that a 'yes, I'll marry you'?"

"It's a definite maybe." Turning her head, she kissed his shoulder.

"Those words are diametrically opposed." He spun her around and locked his arms around her.

Standing on her tiptoes, Sterling set a kiss on his chin and then, diving her hands in his hair, she pulled his mouth down to hers. "One cancels out the other, huh? Then I'll have to choose one?" She pretended to consider the options as she ran her open mouth down his throat, pulled his shirt aside, and ran her tongue across his shoulder.

The sun had moved behind the trees. Night animals began to stir. A stiff breeze played around them.

They were alone. And safe. The last two days were history. Sterling felt a freedom course inside her, felt the anticipation of spending the rest of her life with this man. He was trailing light kisses over her face and talking to her. She didn't understand the words. She didn't need to. Taking his hand, she led him inside.

She sat on the bed and watched as he took off his boots. She let her eyes roam his body as he shed himself of his shirt and jeans. He was magnificent. And he was hers. All hers.

"You could work for Ramsburg with me."

He yanked the T-shirt over her head, laughing. "You should have better taste than to wear a shirt with a saying like that on it." He traced featherlike kisses across her breasts.

"Or you could flip some burgers for Roy. Pick up trash for the sanitary commission. You could be a shoe salesman. With your charm and patience, all the old ladies in town would be swarming in to purchase Nikes. Or . . ." She was silenced when he crushed his mouth to hers and dipped his tongue to taste, to savor.

"Shut up." He rolled her beneath him and she welcomed him.

"I know what. I could become a cop. We could be partners. Hell, we could get a dog and be famous renegade cops. Just think of it. Picture it. Me and you and a dog named Blue."

"I wish I'd met you five years ago," she murmured against his mouth.

"No. You weren't ready for me. I've always been in love with the idea of you. I guess I never really believed I'd feel this way about anyone. It's fate. Sometimes that's all we have."

He rolled to the side and propped his head on his hand. "We're doing something else other than planning our future here, you know." He watched her eyes darken as his lips roamed her face, felt the silkiness of her hands as they roamed over him. Found him.

On a groan, Sterling turned on her side and rubbed his lips with hers. "Say the words, Joe. Say you love me."

He was afraid. Afraid of jinxing everything they had found. Everything she brought him. He was happy before. It was gone in a second. His entire life had been changed in the time it took to draw a breath.

She saw it in his eyes. He still needed a little more

time. She'd give it to him. That and anything else he
needed or wanted. "Okay, Joe. For now. Just show me."

He grabbed her to him and hugged the breath out of
her. Rolling over, he pulled her to lie on top of him. It
was there, in his eyes, in the way he looked at her.

She closed the distance between them.

The next morning she awoke and immediately sensed
he wasn't there beside her.

Sitting straight up in the bed, her eyes darted to every
corner of the room. He was gone.

Throwing back the covers, she got to her feet. Rushing
into the great room, Sterling stopped at the sound coming
from the front porch. Relief had her leaning on the wall
and shaking her head at her own nonsense.

He was on the porch swing, his fingers roaming over
the strings of his guitar.

She padded, barefoot, to stand behind the screen door
and listen.

Joe was shirtless and wearing jeans and boots. His hair
was uncombed and his growth of beard was lengthening.
It was early. The dew freshened the leaves, the grass. The
world looked renewed. She breathed the sweet morning
air and listened to the words he sang, while the hands she
loved so much moved gently and with feeling over the
musical instrument.

His voice was deep and smooth. It was filled with
peace, toned with feelings. His words brought fresh tears
to her eyes and an extra rush of love to her heart.

"You've lived in my mind, you've lived in my heart,
forced by fate to be apart.
I don't have to learn what loving you is, because,
lady, I've loved you for years."

He set the Yamaha against the porch post and leaned
back in the swing. Sterling pushed the screen door open

and walked out. Wiping the tears away, she reached out to touch his shoulder.

"I didn't mean to wake you." He'd wanted to. When he'd awakened he had forced himself to keep from gathering her in his arms again. She needed to sleep, to recover, to be ready to join him completely.

"You didn't. That's a beautiful song."

He nodded. "I wrote it this morning." And adding, after a moment's pause, "It's for you." He looked up at her. "It's been a long time, too long, since I've even been able to pick up the guitar. And I didn't think I'd ever feel like writing a song again. But I woke up this morning and you were lying there beside me, your head resting on my shoulder and the words came." He grinned at her and held his hand out.

She knew that. She had only to listen to the words to know it. She waited just a second before she launched herself into his lap. The swing moved in a wide arch before one side of it crashed from its hooks. The two of them were jolted to the floor and they rolled away, laughter ringing across the air.

He framed her face with his hands. There was freedom in his eyes. She saw it. She tasted it as he kissed her. She listened with her heart as he whispered the words against her lips. "Lady, I've loved you for years."

EPILOGUE

The smell of old books and leather accompanied the odor of ink and Pledge. The lawyer sitting behind the huge cherry desk was dressed in a dark-brown suit, beige shirt, and nondescript tie. His hair was gray. His eyes were watery. His complexion was red. He cleared his throat and drew the attention of those seated in the room.

Sterling had counted nearly twenty people. They were from all walks of life, some young, some old. The clothes ranged from stuffy business suits to jeans; the hairstyles from punk to Fifth Avenue.

She slipped one hand in Joe's free one. His other hand trapped their very active year-old son on his lap. She leaned over to whisper, as the old man began reading the legal jargon. "Vultures. Still all vultures."

Joe bent close to her ear. "If I know John, and I did . . . very well, he's left his entire fortune to charity. I wish I had brought a camera so I could capture the indignities and the shock we'll see today."

Sterling muffled a giggle, since the reading of the will had started and all persons in the room had grown quiet.

Every one of them was waiting to hear their name and the amount of their inheritance. None of these people had seen fit to attend the funeral, though.

She was going to miss John Ramsburg. Her only consolation was that he enjoyed every minute of his adult life. He had taken that life and squeezed it dry. And at seventy-three, he had just lain down and gone to sleep. Bless him. She hoped he wasn't in heaven arguing with the angels or fighting St. Peter for his right to stand at the Pearly Gates and decide who comes in and who doesn't, but she wouldn't put it beyond him.

She became aware of sharp intakes of breath, hushed sounds of surprise and indignation. She made herself pay attention to the boring, droning sounds coming from the attorney.

He read the list of names and the amounts, which ranged from one dollar to five. Each and every relative had been mentioned and then scalped. Sterling smiled. It was what Ramsburg called comeuppance. Then Sterling heard her name mentioned.

"And to Mr. and Mrs. Joe MacDaniels and their son, Johnny, I leave my entire estate, to be used for the persuit of happiness of others and the continuation of their very own personal joy. Since I am being divorced from life, it is only fitting there should be some sort of a settlement. Sterling, you wanted to know my secret. You always wanted to know who had given me that second chance. I never knew his proper name. He found me alongside the road when I was fifteen. I had been hitchhiking and was picked up by some so-called friends. After they beat me up and robbed me of the twelve dollars I had in my pocket, they left me on the side of the road. Another passerby stopped, took me home, gave me time to rest and recover. When I left his small shack by the railroad tracks I knew him only as Bill. He couldn't read or write. He was poor and had nothing but an old harmonica that he made great sounds come out of. Three states away, I finally had time to rest. When I undressed, I found that a small pouch had been roughly sewn into the lining of my old jacket. It contained several hundred dollars. The old man had no use for the money. He was happy just the way he was, but he wanted me to have it, to have a chance to be better than those who had beat me up. I began to make my fortune and I went back for Bill, but he was dead. I never had a chance to say thank you. So keep looking, Sterling. Keep helping in the same tradition; and now you have a secret of your own. And I'll see you later."

The lawyer stopped and glanced up. People squirmed in their seats. He didn't hear shrieks of joy, only the indignant grunts of the rest of the people in the room.

Sterling and Joe turned their surprised faces toward each other and smiled. Sterling dabbed at her eyes with a lacy handkerchief. Bless him. Bless all those like him.

Joe slipped an arm around Sterling. "I think we better make a hasty exit. The natives are getting restless."

She was determined not to show a tear to this crowd. "So, he finally chose to let me in on the mystery. And all that money. I begged him not to do it. I never thought he really would. I don't know if I like all that responsibility."

"Learn to live with it." Joe offered her his hand.

She stood up and made her way through the milling people, all of whom were ignoring the lawyer's final statements. She bent over to Joe as they walked through the doorway. "I'm going to miss that man. I'm glad our little Johnny was able to spend some time with him. They sure had a lot of good times together."

The sunlight hit them and little Johnny dipped his face to hide in his father's jacket, gurgling happily. Joe stopped her with a hand on her arm. "Shall we take the BMW or the Mercedes convertible?"

Catching up with his little game, she hugged his arm to her. "Since we're going to the cabin for a few days, I suggest we take the Jeep. You still haven't gotten that road straightened out . . ."

SHARE THE FUN . . .
SHARE YOUR NEW-FOUND TREASURE!!

You don't want to let your new books out of your sight? That's okay. Your friends can get their own. Order below.

No. 41 SPIDER'S WEB by Allie Jordan
Silvia's life was quiet and organized until Fletcher arrived on her doorstep. Will life ever be the same?

No. 42 TRUE COLORS by Dixie DuBois
Julian has the power to crush Nikki's world with the bat of an eye. But can he help her save herself? Can he save himself from Nikki?

No. 43 DUET by Patricia Collinge
On stage, Adam and Marina fit together like two pieces of a puzzle. Love just might be the glue that keeps them together off stage, as well.

No. 44 DEADLY COINCIDENCE by Denise Richards
J.D.'s instincts tell him he can't be wrong about his beautiful Laurie; her heart says to trust him. If they're wrong, it could be deadly!

No. 45 PERSONAL BEST by Margaret Watson
Nick is a cynic; Tess, an optimist. Where does love fit in?

No. 46 ONE ON ONE by JoAnn Barbour
Vincent's no saint but Loie's attracted to the devil in him anyway.

No. 47 STERLING'S REASONS by Joey Light
Joe is running from his conscience; Sterling helps him find peace.

No. 48 SNOW SOUNDS by Heather Williams
In the quiet of the mountain, Tanner and Melaine find each other again.
